Praise for the Midnight Breed series by LARA ADRIAN

BOUND TO DARKNESS

"While most series would have ended or run out of steam, the Midnight Breed series seems to have picked up steam. Lara Adrian has managed to keep the series fresh by adding new characters . . . without having to say goodbye to the original ones that made the series so popular to begin with. Bound to Darkness has all the passion, danger and unique appeal of the original ten books but also stands on its own as a turning point in the entire series with new pieces to a larger puzzle, new friends and old enemies."

—*Adria's Romance Reviews*

"Lara Adrian always manages to write great love stories, not only emotional but action packed. I love every aspect of (Bound to Darkness). I also enjoyed how we get a glimpse into the life of the other characters we have come to love. There is always something sexy and erotic in all of Adrian's books, making her one of my top 5 paranormal authors."

—*Reading Diva*

CRAVE THE NIGHT

"Nothing beats good writing and that is what ultimately makes Lara Adrian stand out amongst her peers.... Crave the Night is stunning in its flawless execution. Lara Adrian has the rare ability to lure readers right into her books, taking them on a ride they will never forget."

—*Under the Covers*

"...Steamy and intense. This installment is sure to delight established fans and will also be accessible to new readers."

—*Publishers Weekly*

EDGE OF DAWN

"Adrian's strikingly original Midnight Breed series delivers an abundance of nail-biting suspenseful chills, red-hot sexy thrills, an intricately built world, and realistically complicated and conflicted protagonists, whose happily-ever-after ending proves to be all the sweeter after what they endure to get there."

—*Booklist (starred review)*

DARKER AFTER MIDNIGHT

"A riveting novel that will keep readers mesmerized… If you like romance combined with heart-stopping paranormal suspense, you're going to love this book."

—*Bookpage*

DEEPER THAN MIDNIGHT

"One of the consistently best paranormal series out there…. Adrian writes compelling individual stories (with wonderful happily ever afters) within a larger story arc that is unfolding with a refreshing lack of predictability."

—*Romance Novel News*

Praise for Lara Adrian

"With an Adrian novel, readers are assured of plenty of dangerous thrills and passionate chills."

—*RT Book Reviews*

"Ms. Adrian has a gift for drawing her readers deeper and deeper into the amazing world she creates."

—*Fresh Fiction*

Praise for the 100 Series contemporary erotic romance from
LARA ADRIAN

"There are twists that I want to say that I expect from a Lara Adrian book, and I say that because with any Adrian book you read, you know there's going to be a complex storyline. Adrian simply does billionaires better."

–*Under the Covers*

"I have been searching and searching for the next book boyfriend to leave a lasting impression. You know the ones: where you own the paperbacks, eBooks and the audible versions…This is that book. For those of you who are looking for your next Fifty Fix, look no further. I know, I know–you have heard the phrase before! Except this time, it's the truth and I will bet the penthouse on it."

—*Mile High Kink Book Club*

"I wish I could give this more than 5 stars! Lara Adrian not only dips her toe into this genre with flare, she will take it over . . . I have found my new addiction, this series."

–*The Sub Club Books*

"If you're looking for a hot new contemporary romance along the lines of Sylvia Day's Crossfire series then you're not going to want to miss this series!"

–*Feeling Fictional*

Look for these titles in the *New York Times* and #1 international bestselling

Midnight Breed series

A Touch of Midnight (prequel novella)
Kiss of Midnight
Kiss of Crimson
Midnight Awakening
Midnight Rising
Veil of Midnight
Ashes of Midnight
Shades of Midnight
Taken by Midnight
Deeper Than Midnight
A Taste of Midnight (ebook novella)
Darker After Midnight
The Midnight Breed Series Companion
Edge of Dawn
Marked by Midnight (novella)
Crave the Night
Tempted by Midnight (novella)
Bound to Darkness
Stroke of Midnight (novella)
Defy the Dawn
Midnight Untamed (novella)
Midnight Unbound (novella)
Midnight Unleashed (novella)
Claimed in Shadows
Break the Day
Fall of Night
King of Midnight (Fall 2021)

Other books by Lara Adrian

Paranormal Romance

Hunter Legacy Series
Born of Darkness
Hour of Darkness
Edge of Darkness

Contemporary Romance

100 Series
For 100 Days
For 100 Nights
For 100 Reasons

100 Series Standalones
Run to You
Play My Game

Historical Romance

Dragon Chalice Series
Heart of the Hunter
Heart of the Flame
Heart of the Dove

Warrior Trilogy
White Lion's Lady
Black Lion's Bride
Lady of Valor

Lord of Vengeance

FALL OF NIGHT

A Midnight Breed Novel

NEW YORK TIMES BESTSELLING AUTHOR
LARA ADRIAN

ISBN: 9798701578799

FALL OF NIGHT
© 2021 by Lara Adrian, LLC
Cover design © 2020 by CrocoDesigns

All rights reserved. No part of this work may be used or reproduced in any manner whatsoever without permission, except in the case of brief quotations embodied in critical articles and reviews.

This book is a work of fiction. Names, characters, places and incidents are either products of the author's imagination or used fictitiously. Any resemblance to actual events, locales, or persons, living or dead, is entirely coincidental. No part of this publication can be reproduced or transmitted in any form or by any means, electronic or mechanical, without permission in writing from the Author.

www.LaraAdrian.com

Available in ebook and trade paperback. Unabridged audiobook edition forthcoming.

FALL OF NIGHT

CHAPTER 1

☪

It was the silence that disturbed her the most.
Not the black, moonless night sky overhead. Not the hours she'd spent wandering alone in that darkness, trying to find her way through an endless stretch of scorched forest and barren earth. No, it was the complete and utter stillness that made her blood run cold in her veins.

The deadness of the place chilled her to her bones. It seeped into her marrow like poison, like a warning, as her feet navigated the cinders and dead foliage on the ground.

Phaedra didn't scare easily. None of her immortal kind did. Yet she couldn't deny her urgency to leave this place. Her heart hammered with that need, the only sound she heard in the maddening quiet surrounding her.

Out of old habit, she reached for the bracelet on her wrist. She'd worn the leather thong with its small piece of precious Atlantean crystal for as long as she could recall. The amulet could teleport her away in an instant. But her wrist was bare. She'd given the bracelet to her friend Tamisia weeks ago, never imagining she might need it herself.

Phaedra was on her own here. All she could do now was push on.

The wasteland maze of denuded, skeletal trees only seemed to expand the more she tried to escape it. One jagged path turned into another, then another. Straight trails morphed into circular loops that carried her nowhere. Clearings she thought she was heading toward instead moved farther away before dissolving altogether, nothing more than mirages.

Frustration gnawed at her.

There had to be a way out. She just needed to keep going until she found it.

Against the pitch-dark night, a pale shape emerged from behind a cluster of gnarled, blackened trees several yards away.

A doe.

Graceful, calm, as white as milk, she stepped out to the broken path ahead of Phaedra. Dark, placid eyes blinked once in acknowledgment, no trace of fear in the animal's gentle face. It waited, its breath softly misting in the chill night air.

"Hello, there," Phaedra whispered.

She didn't dare move, loath to spook the beautiful creature. All the anxiousness of her frantic trek through the alien landscape faded under the doe's comforting presence.

"Where did you come from? Are you lost like me?"

Carefully, she took a measured step forward. The doe retreated a step.

Phaedra immediately paused, frowning in disappointment. "Please, don't be afraid of me."

The deer backed up farther. Then she calmly turned around and began to step back into the lifeless forest.

Phaedra followed. The doe kept an ample distance between them, but she didn't bolt. She didn't abandon Phaedra to the wasteland. Instead, she seemed to be leading her somewhere. Guiding her toward something.

Not out of the forsaken woods, but deeper into them.

The twisted trees grew thicker the farther she followed the animal, the scorched bracken at her feet more tangled and forbidding.

"No."

Phaedra wasn't sure if she spoke the word aloud or voiced it only in her head. The doe glanced back at her, halting in the darkness. There seemed to be a question in the soft eyes, an entreaty.

Phaedra shook her head, her long brown hair stirring in the night breeze. "I'm not going any farther."

She waited for the animal to resume its retreat into the forest. She fully expected the unusual creature to disappear like the apparition she was certain it must be.

But the doe didn't leave.

Slowly, it approached her.

It stepped toward her with serene purpose, until it stood close enough for Phaedra to touch.

She couldn't resist the temptation to brush her fingertips over the gleaming white coat. The fur felt like velvet under her hand, the steady pound of the doe's heartbeat a reassurance Phaedra didn't even realize she needed until the vibration of it thrummed beneath her fingers.

Those gentle, fathomless brown eyes spoke of eons of wisdom.

And something more elusive that Phaedra yearned to understand.

"Why are you here?" She stroked her fingertips over the doe's smooth brow and delicate snout. "I wish you could tell me wh—"

Phaedra's words stuck in her throat. Somewhere behind her, the stillness of the wasteland forest shifted. It breathed.

Only the smallest change in the air, imperceptible, except to someone with her inhumanly acute senses. Her skin prickled at the feeling of unease that washed over her. She let her hand fall away from the white doe, slowly pivoting her head to listen closer, to scan the skeletal landscape for the intruders she instinctively knew were there.

Men.

She didn't see them yet; she felt them.

But that couldn't be right.

Why would anyone be in this forsaken place? What could they want?

Whatever their reasons, their presence here wasn't good. They moved on silent feet, carrying the scent of violence and weaponry on them. And they were coming closer every second.

Phaedra now caught a glimpse of their dark shapes moving between the scorched trees in the distance behind her. At least four of them, maybe more. The group began to split up and fan out with military precision.

With a whisper of warning at the tip of her tongue, Phaedra turned back to the gentle white doe to urge it to run with her for safety.

It was gone.

Vanished without a sound or a trace.

She only wished she could disappear too. Glancing behind her, she gauged the oncoming danger. The largest of the soldiers, the one in the lead, abruptly halted the others with a sharp upward slash of his black-gloved hand as he peered in her direction.

Oh, no.

He'd spotted her.

Although she couldn't see his face beneath the black head covering and smudges of grease meant to further camouflage him in the dark, she felt the clash of his gaze as it slammed into hers across the distance. The force of that connection pushed her back on her heels. It zinged through her veins like a lick of lightning, making the fine hairs on her arms and at her nape stand on end.

He wasn't human. Not Atlantean, either.

Breed. The longtime enemy of her people. The blood-drinking, lethal offspring of the savage otherworlders who nearly succeeded in wiping out all of Atlantis many millennia ago.

That unerring stare locked on to her, the immense warrior broke away from the rest of his group and started for her through the bracken.

Phaedra started running.

Without her amulet to fly her home, she had no other choice but to flee and pray she might be faster than the heavily armed soldier at her heels.

His boots crunched in the cinders and dead foliage on the ground behind her. Brittle branches snapped like gunfire as he crashed through them.

He was going to catch her; she had no doubt about that. What he meant to do with her once he had, she didn't want to guess.

She ran harder, drawing on all the preternatural speed she could muster.

And still he kept coming. The chase pushed them deeper into the wasteland, the rest of the warrior's companions far behind them now.

"Stop," he called out to her, his deep voice tight with urgency.

Phaedra kept running. She didn't know where she was headed, nor how long she could manage to go before the dangerous Breed male caught her. The only thing she knew for certain was the need to get as far away from this place as she possibly could.

She heard him gaining on her. She felt the sheer strength and power of the male as his booted feet chewed up the distance between them.

Faith, help her. She couldn't hope to outpace him. Though she wasn't helpless—far from it.

Pure Atlantean blood coursed through her veins. She felt the heat of it rising inside her with every frantic step she took. Her palms tingled, already beginning to glow at her sides.

From behind her, the warrior's words grated in a hiss. "Damn it, female, I said stop running."

She sensed the instant he leapt into the air at her back, but it still came as a visceral shock to see him land on the ground right in front of her.

Phaedra jolted to a halt, her breath heaving. As tall as she was, this Breed male towered over her by several inches. Hulking shoulders and muscled limbs moved with the predatory grace of a big cat.

"Who are you?" he demanded.

The gaze that had skewered her across the distance when he first spotted her was no less arresting up close. His eyes were too beautiful on the face of a male built for war. The stormy shade of lavender burned away as she stared at him, amber sparks lighting his irises with unearthly fire.

"Answer me." Full, sculpted lips peeled back from gleaming white teeth and long fangs. "Who are you? What are you doing out here?"

Phaedra edged backward. "I could ask you the same thing."

His lips flattened. "It's not safe for you."

She didn't think this awful stretch of deadness could be safe for anyone, possibly not even this dangerous male or his comrades. "What is this place?"

"You don't know?" A flicker of confusion softened the hard edge of his suspicion, but only for a moment. He glanced down at her hands and a tendon jerked in his jaw. She could feel the glow in her palms increasing under his scrutiny. He cocked his head. His eyes glowed now, filled with amber fire and suspicion. "Holy shit. You're one of them."

He took a step toward her.

"Stay back." Phaedra brought her hands up in front of her like a shield.

More than a shield, they were a terrible weapon. The Atlantean light she carried inside her was a fearsome power, one she was loathe to wield, especially when this Breed warrior hadn't threatened her with any harm.

Yet.

He reached out a black-gloved hand. "You're coming with me."

"Don't move any closer or I'll—"

Far from afraid, he bit off an incredulous-sounding curse, his teeth and fangs flashing white in the moonless night. "Or you'll what?"

Faith, she didn't know what she'd do. Nor did she have the chance to respond.

All at once, the inky night sky exploded. Blinding white light erupted all around them.

Unearthly light.

Not from her, but not of the mortal world, either. Phaedra closed her eyes, but it did little to block the blast of illumination behind her eyelids. The power of it buffeted her, taking her legs out from beneath her.

She felt herself flying backward, yanked by an invisible hand. She waited to feel her body crash down onto the hard forest floor. Instead she was still in motion, pulled backward even faster, as though caught in a vortex.

Somewhere, growing ever more distant, the sound of men's screams shook the lifeless forest.

Agonized screams. The sounds of indescribable suffering.

Was the lavender-eyed warrior among the tortured and dying?

For reasons she didn't understand, the thought that he might be sent an arc of pain like a dagger into her breast.

"No!" Phaedra felt the cry erupt inside her, but it stayed trapped in the back of her throat. Caught in that invisible grasp that hauled her backward, she couldn't speak at all. She tumbled through an endless chasm, the sounds of annihilation still ringing in her ears.

The anguish of it raked her to her soul.

"No . . . no. No!"

"Phaedra?" Soft pressure landed on her shoulders, giving her a little shake. "Phay, wake up."

Her eyelids flew up and she found herself blinking up into the sky-blue eyes of her friend, Tamisia. The platinum-blonde Atlantean female frowned, her beautiful face filled with worry. "Are you all right?"

"What? Oh, yes. I—I'm fine." Phaedra sat up in her chair, embarrassed by her outburst. "I'm sorry, I must've dozed off."

She and Sia had been enjoying some tea and a light lunch on the rooftop garden area of Phaedra's little house in Rome before her friend had stepped away to take a call from her mate, Trygg. She couldn't have been gone for more than a few minutes, yet it was evidently long enough for Phaedra to drop into a thick sleep.

A disturbing and awful one.

Sia lowered herself into the chair next to Phaedra. "That must've been some nightmare. You're as pale as a sheet."

Phaedra swallowed. "I dreamt about the scorched forest again, and the white doe."

For more than a week now, it had been a recurring theme every time she laid her head down to sleep. The dream had played out roughly unaltered, until now.

"It started the same way it always does," she murmured, still caught in the weblike strands of her sleep. "I followed the doe into the charred woods, but someone else was there too. Sia, the dream changed into something terrible this time. And all of it felt so real."

"Do you want to tell me about it?"

"No." Phaedra shook her head. The anguish of what she'd heard and imagined behind her closed eyelids as the wasteland went bright with annihilating power was still too fresh in her senses. She didn't want to think about it any longer, much less try to put the nightmare into words. "It was just a silly dream, that's all. I don't want you thinking your friend has gone mad."

Tamisia's gaze was sympathetic, her expression gentle with concern. "Do you want to know what I really think? You're working too hard, Phay. Running the shelter here at the house is a twenty-four hour obligation. It's too much for just one person to handle, even for you."

"It's not work," Phaedra insisted. "Looking after the women and children who come here looking for safety and protection never feels like an obligation to me."

"I know it doesn't." Sia knew that better than most.

Very recently, she had helped Phaedra run the shelter for a few weeks after Sia had been exiled from the Atlantean colony where she'd once been a high-ranking member of the Council of Elders. Sia's misplaced alliance with one of the colony's own had cost her dearly, but she had since redeemed herself. Now, she lived at the Order's compound in Rome with Trygg, the Breed warrior she'd fallen in love with and taken as her mate.

For Phaedra, an immortal who'd lived for as many countless centuries as her friend, the shelter had become her life's purpose.

It was all she had left in this world.

"I'm perfectly fine, Tamisia. Please, don't worry about me."

"I'm your friend. Worrying about you comes with the territory." She placed a tender hand on Phaedra's arm. "You need a break. Actually, what you really need is a full-time assistant here at the shelter. I'd be more than happy to help you find someone trustworthy and qualified. In fact, I'll manage the shelter myself while you're gone."

"No. It's really not necessary."

"It's the least I can do for you, and besides, I've already worked with most of the residents. They know me. And if anything should come up, between Trygg and me, I'm sure we can handle it."

"I appreciate the offer, Sia, but—"

"Wonderful. Then it's settled." Sia gave her a look that invited no argument.

While Phaedra had once been part of the Atlantean royal court with her parents, those days were long past. Tamisia had only been exiled from her station as an Elder for a matter of months, and it showed in her unwavering gaze.

"First, we'll have our tea and lunch, and you can tell me what happened in the dream this time," Sia said. "Then we'll start making plans for you to take a well-deserved, and much needed, break. Someplace relaxing and stress-free."

Phaedra knew better than to argue once Tamisia had made up her mind about something. And she had to admit, if even to herself, that the idea of getting away from the crowds and bustle of Rome for short time did sound appealing. She wasn't sure where she might want to go, nor did it matter.

Wherever she went now, she knew nothing would ever deliver her from the soul-shredding cries of the men who had perished so horrifically in the terrible light of her dream.

CHAPTER 2

☾

One week later...

The translator seemed nervous.

Tegan wasn't sure if the young Kazakhstani looked ready to piss himself because of what he was hearing from the wary old man he spoke with, or because of the big, scowling vampire waiting impatiently to receive the troubling news.

Tegan's brows furrowed even deeper, his fangs prickling in his gums. He was in no mood for roadblocks or delays. He'd been gone from his home and his beloved mate back in the States for close to seven days now. His boots had covered countless miles of rough terrain, starting in Budapest where the missing Order warriors had last been heard from, then through the forested taiga of Siberian Russia where the team's secret mission had abruptly lost all contact.

A combination of instinct, logic, and desperate guessing had brought him down into neighboring Kazakhstan last night. He'd waited out the daylight hours in Petropavl, a small city just across the border. With a train station and a university nearby, there had been plenty of humans around to provide him with the sustenance he'd sorely needed.

As a Gen One Breed, Tegan had to feed every few days. After trekking alone for at least that long through the Russian wilderness, he'd been half-starved by the time he finally sank his fangs into the throat of a young thug who'd had the bad sense to try to pick his pocket outside the station after nightfall.

It wasn't until Tegan had taken his fill of fresh red cells from the thug's carotid that he noticed the unusual weapon that had clattered out of the human's hand. The long dagger was too well-made to belong to a common street hood, especially one who likely hadn't ventured more than a few hundred kilometers away from the remote city or the barren steppes of his homeland.

No, the blade was not some crude weapon. It was beautiful, and crafted of something more than pedestrian steel. Hand-forged titanium.

The kind of weapon that belonged to a Breed warrior.

When Tegan saw the tooled grip that had been custom-fitted to the hand of the Order member who'd carried it, every cell in his body lit up with recognition—and with a cold dread he refused to acknowledge.

No warrior in the Order would ever willingly surrender his blade. Most especially, not the formidable male who had lost this one.

Tegan hadn't needed to pick up the blade to know that it would fit his own large hand nearly perfectly.

After all, it had been made for his son, Micah.

He glowered at the thug he'd pressed into service as his translator back in Petropavl, who was currently asking questions on Tegan's behalf. "What's the old man telling you? You said you bought that blade off him three days ago. Where the fuck did he get it?"

Both humans flinched at his biting tone. No doubt, the glint of his elongating fangs in the dim light of the round, tent-like yurt didn't give either man much comfort.

Good. His patience had been threadbare even before he arrived in this desolate patch of flat grasslands in Kazakhstan's north country. Each second that kept him away from the truth about Micah's blade only made his fury simmer closer to a boil.

The gray-haired man seated on the rug in the center of the candlelit tent was the patriarch of the clan of nomad herders temporarily camped on the steppe. They had set up there to let their sheep and cattle graze on the yellowed grasses before autumn turned to brutal winter.

The makeshift village was comprised of fewer than a dozen similar yurts. Outside the one where Tegan braced for bad news, nervous livestock bayed and snuffled, instinctively aware of the presence of the apex predator in their midst. A predator who was growing increasingly dangerous by the second.

The pair of humans staring at Tegan showed similar anxiety as the animals.

"The dagger," he growled. "Where did the old man get it?"

The translator swallowed. "He says it came from a wanderer who showed up here in the camp last week. He was gravely wounded, traveling alone on foot. The old man says the wanderer was a . . . one of your kind."

Tegan let a curse slip through his clenched teeth. He didn't want to think the injured Breed male could have been his son, but the alternative was a cold comfort too. What might have happened to Micah to separate him from his teammates? He was their captain, a devoted soldier who would never abandon his comrades under any circumstances.

Just as Tegan was certain his son would never surrender his blade unless he was too weak to hold it. Or worse.

Those were thoughts he refused to consider.

"Tell the old man I need more information. Did the wanderer say anything—anything at all? What kind of injuries did he have? Where had he come from? How long was he here at the camp?"

The young Kazakh's dark eyes were grim as he slowly shook his head. "He's said all he knows about the stranger. His path ended here the same night he arrived. Not long afterward, he closed his eyes and never opened them again. I am . . . sorry."

A sudden anguish seeped into Tegan's veins, into his heart. He'd set out on this search determined to find his missing son and the Order team Micah had been leading. He'd told himself he would not rest until he had succeeded.

Worse than that, he had promised Elise nothing bad would happen to their son. He'd sworn it as an oath, not only to her but to himself as he'd stared into her beautiful, fear-stricken lavender eyes and made that vow.

Now, those words settled on his tongue like ashes.

He wasn't ready to acknowledge what he was hearing. Christ, he'd never be ready for that.

"What did the old man do afterward . . . What did they do with his body?" The question sounded detached from him, wooden words that he could barely choke out.

The translator turned to the nomad elder to ask in their language. The exchange took longer than it should have, a rushed back-and-forth that seemed to stir confusion in the younger man.

Tegan stared, irritated to be left out of the conversation. "What's wrong? What is he saying?"

Frowning, the Kazakh glanced back at Tegan. "There is no body. The wanderer . . . he didn't die."

Tegan growled. "You just told me—"

"Yes, yes, I know what I said. But the dialect of this region is tricky." He shook his head. "The stranger came here with grievous wounds. He was very weak. He collapsed and has not regained consciousness."

"You mean, he's alive?"

The translator nodded. "They are keeping him in one of the yurts here at the camp. The old man says they've tried to look after him as best they can, but he grows weaker by the hour. His care exceeds what they're able to give him."

A wild hope surged inside Tegan, but he bit it back. Until he saw his son with his own eyes—until he confirmed that the injured warrior truly was Micah—there was no room to let down his guard. "Take me to him. Now."

The translator communicated the command to the nomad elder. With a sober nod, the sheepherder got up from his seat on the rug. Bent, slow-moving, he motioned for them to follow him out of the yurt.

Tegan's heart drummed as he walked impatiently behind the pair of humans along the tread-worn path between the rest of the small camp. A few curious heads peeked out of the tents to watch them pass, whispers and murmurs buzzing in Tegan's wake.

The Breed had been known to their human cohabitants of this planet for more than twenty years, though hardly welcomed by the masses. That this remote clan had taken care of one of his kind at a time of need was a miracle Tegan never would have expected. It did more than surprise him. It humbled him.

Yet none of that prepared him for what awaited inside the dark yurt at the end of the encampment.

As they approached, the sickly stench of looming death assaulted him like a hammer driven into the center of his chest. Once inside, the reality hit him even harder. The rasp of shallow, irregular breathing made the air in his own lungs seize up. The sight of the large, yet obviously diminished, shape of the Breed male lying on the thin cot in the center of the yurt sent cold dread leeching into his veins.

The old man turned on a battery-powered lantern that sat on a low table near the entrance. The glow illuminated the tent, but Tegan's Breed vision didn't need the light in order to recognize that he was looking at his son.

"Ah, fuck." The words gusted out of him on a choked breath.

He moved to the side of the meager bed and stared down at Micah, fear and a father's indescribable pain filling the space behind his sternum.

"Son." The word was raw in his throat. "Micah, can you hear me?"

No response, not even a flinch of the dark lashes resting on his ashen cheeks. Tegan took hold of Micah's big hand, clasping the cool, heavy fingers between his warmer ones, rubbing them to create friction as he prayed for some kind of signal that his son would be all right.

Beneath the sheet and animal pelt that covered Micah's body, the strong, formidable young warrior slept without stirring.

"How many days has he been in this coma?" Tegan asked the question without glancing away from the only child he had. Now that he had his eyes on him, he couldn't bear to look away—no matter how wrenching it was to see such a force of nature laid low by what had clearly been catastrophic injuries.

The old man and the younger one spoke briefly behind him in their language. "This was the fourth day," the translator said. "The fifth night starts tonight."

Four full days. No wonder there was barely anything left of him. It was likely only Micah's second-generation Breed genetics that had let him survive the severity of his wounds at all. Those same genetics would be the thing to finish him if he was allowed to waste away any longer without proper care.

Or without the blood his body needed in order to heal.

Tegan unsheathed his son's dagger, then glanced over his shoulder at the younger of the two humans. "Come here."

"W-what do you mean to do with that?" Panic edged the stammered question. "I did what you asked. I brought you here. I got you the answers you wanted. Please . . . please, don't kill me."

"I said step forward."

The Kazakh shuffled closer, looking less of the cocky thug from the city and more like the terrified coward he truly was. As soon as he was within reach, Tegan took him by the forearm and hauled him next to Micah on the bed.

He gave him a flash of his fangs. "Relax. I'm not going to kill you."

He sliced the edge of the titanium blade across the human's wrist. Blood surged from the wound, dark crimson and thick with life-giving red cells. The young man howled, but Tegan knew it was only out of fear. He held the open wound over Micah's slack mouth, willing his son to take some of the nourishment that ran over his lips and down his squared chin.

"Hold still," he told the squirming human. He would mind scrub him of their entire encounter once Micah had taken what he needed.

If he would take it.

"Come on, son. Drink," Tegan murmured. Resheathing the dagger, he used his free hand to open Micah's mouth.

It wasn't going to work.

The fresh blood pooled on his tongue, only a few drops making it down his throat.

If he couldn't swallow, he couldn't drink.

And if he couldn't drink, he was going to die.

Either way, Tegan had to get him out of there.

With a growl, he pulled the man's wrist to his mouth and sealed the wound with a swipe of his tongue. The bleeding stopped at once, the skin healing over almost instantly.

The young Kazakh scrambled away from him, sputtering something in his native language as he stared at his vanishing injury.

Tegan stood up and walked over to the old man who had given Micah shelter and care these past few crucial days and nights. There was a wariness in the dark eyes that stared back at him, but there seemed to be an understanding, even sympathy, in the old patriarch's lined face. Understanding that needed no translation.

Tegan extended his hand. "Thank you for looking after my son."

The aged human reached out, his grasp surprisingly firm as he gave a nod of acknowledgment.

While the younger Kazakh continued to inspect his wrist and hyperventilate on the other side of the tent, Tegan strode to Micah's bedside and took out the satellite phone he'd carried with him since leaving the States. He would need to call Elise and let her know he'd found their son.

But first, he needed to make arrangements to get him home.

He punched in the code that connected him to a secured line at the Order's Washington, D.C., headquarters.

"I have him," he told Lucan Thorne, the founder of the Order and Tegan's oldest friend. "I've got Micah."

The exhalation on the other end of the line was filled with relief. "And the rest of his team?"

"Just Micah. He's in bad shape. It doesn't look good for the others, Lucan." He glanced down at Micah on the cot, his slack lips stained with the blood he desperately needed but had barely absorbed. "Ah, fuck, Lucan. It doesn't look good for my son, either."

"We're on it," Lucan replied, his low voice grim but steady with resolve. "We've already got your coordinates. Gideon's making arrangements to have a medevac team on the ground to pick you up ASAP."

"Thanks."

"No thanks required. You ought to know that by now, brother."

Yeah, he did. Tegan fell silent, unable to express how much he needed to hear his friend's reassurances. In the background, he heard the traces of Gideon's British accent as he spoke and the clack of his fingers typing on a computer keyboard.

"Gideon says Lazaro Archer's already responded to the call," Lucan said. "He's dispatching one of his units from Rome as we speak."

"Okay." Tegan stole another look at his son. He couldn't hold back the jagged sigh that tore out of him. "And Lucan? Tell Lazaro to hurry."

CHAPTER 3

☾

Ash clung to the back of his parched throat. Micah tried to swallow, but his jaw felt rusted tight. His tongue was thick, his mouth as dry as a desert. He groaned, and was shocked to hear the low sound vibrate deep in his chest.

He was alive?

Fuck.

Pain in his lungs as he choked in a gasping breath wrenched his crusted eyelids open, but only for a second. His retinas felt aflame, still seared from the explosion of light that had come out of nowhere and lit up the ghostly forest brighter than the midday sun.

He could still see his fallen teammates after he'd rushed back to find them. Or, rather, what little had been left of them.

All five Breed warriors who had served with him in their elite unit of the Order, gone.

Nothing but cinders and melted weapons near the epicenter of the unearthly blast.

As their captain, his men would have followed him into any battle—and had—no matter the risk. Instead, the impulse that had pushed Micah to command the team deeper into the wastelands of the Siberian interior had led them into a trap he never saw coming.

He should have stayed on course.

They'd had their orders. They had carried out their mission with flawless precision. When it was done, he should have taken his team back to base. Instead, he'd felt a prickling at the back of his neck, as if the harsh forest terrain whispered to him. Beckoned him deeper. Kept pulling him forward until the taiga gave way to a woodland of skeletal, lifeless trees that seemed to stretch on for miles and miles.

He knew the place, even though he'd never stepped foot there. It was crazy. Hell, maybe he was fucking crazy.

That's what he'd thought when he spotted the white doe that had emerged out of the charred trees. He'd seen it before, but this time it was real. So was the woman accompanying the ethereal animal. She, too, had materialized amid the barren woods like a vision. Tall and slender, yet mouth-wateringly feminine, she'd stopped him dead in his tracks.

He, the skilled warrior, the disciplined captain who had earned his rank through punishing training and unflinching focus on his orders and his duty, had left his men to run after her, curiosity only part of what drew him to her. Then, after he'd caught up to her, like an idiot he'd stood frozen in confusion—and in pure primal response—to the chestnut-haired beauty who seemed to have dropped into the center of his world like something out of a fantasy.

Right up until the moment when he saw her glowing hands and realized what she was.

Atlantean.

The immortal race whose queen, Selene, had declared them at war with all of the Breed and mankind alike.

Micah and his team had gone willingly to the front lines of that mounting war, but he never expected the kind of ambush that had confronted them in the middle of that Siberian wasteland.

He thought it had all been a dream.

He'd nearly had himself convinced it was all just a terrible, unspeakable dream. A nightmare of shock, agony . . . and guilt.

One that had been followed by a black, bottomless oblivion that had taken hold of him and seemed to last for an eternity.

Now, with his senses slowly coming back online, he realized it was worse than a nightmare.

It had been real.

His team was dead.

Their mission had ended in disaster.

And him? He'd rather be ashes on the ground along with his Order comrades than live and have to carry the weight of failing them so unforgivably.

Groaning again, he cracked open his lids and breathed through the sensation of hot daggers piercing his eyeballs.

Maybe this was hell. Maybe he'd finally reached the floor of the pit that had been sucking him down and this was where he'd spend the rest of forever, reliving his shame and agony.

His vision was bleary at best, even in the cool darkness of the room where he lay. Dim memories of musty tent walls and the stench of livestock and campfires seemed out of place as he tried to take note of his current surroundings.

A soft pillow cushioned his head. Underneath his battered, depleted body was a narrow bed with a comfortable mattress and crisp white sheets. Monitoring wires were taped to his chest, arms, and hands. Next to the bed, medical equipment beeped and hummed.

Not hell, then.

A hospital room.

But that didn't seem right, either. No hospital was of any use to one of the Breed. The only thing that could heal his kind was blood. Fresh red cells, taken from an open human vein.

And Christ, he was starving.

Pushing himself up off the mattress felt like trying to move through hardening concrete. His limbs felt as though they hadn't been used for a year. Every muscle in his body screamed with every inch of movement he managed.

How long had he been in this place?

How the hell did he get there?

In the back of his mind, he could almost hear his father's deep voice urging him to hang on, reassuring him that he would be all right.

Impossible, considering Tegan was back in the States with Micah's mother, Elise, and the rest of the Order.

Micah hadn't seen any of them for some long weeks. Not since he and his unit had deployed to Budapest. The way he felt right now, that black ops assignment could have been years ago.

Micah slowly swung his legs over the edge of the mattress and paused to catch his breath. Someone had been taking care of him, as much as they could, anyway. His combat gear and weapons had been removed at some point. Barefoot and bare-chested, he was dressed only in a pair of loose-fitting gray sweats. His skin had been cleaned of the blistering and the blood and the sweat that clung to him as he'd dragged himself out of the Siberian taiga.

Thanks to his Breed genetics, the worst of his wounds were mending, but too slowly. If he didn't feed soon, the burns would be the least of his concerns.

His vision still burned, even in the low light of the room. Fever from his thirst painted everything in shades of red. Glancing down at his hands where they rested atop his thighs, he watched the colors of his dermaglyphs churn and roil in all the shades of hunger.

The deep purples and dark reds edged dangerously close to black—the stage at which he would have little to no control over the ferocity of his need for blood.

By the look of his glyphs and the gnawing hollowness of his body, he couldn't be more than a few hours away from that edge.

He had a choice to make.

Lie back down and wait to join his comrades in death, or get up and fight to live.

Live to avenge them, by doing whatever it would take to bring down Selene and all who serve her.

That was enough to live for.

Hell, it was more than enough reason.

Reaching up, he tore the monitoring wires away from his chest. The ones on his arms and hands came off next. He tossed the leads in a tangle on the narrow bed as he pushed himself up to his feet and tested the shaky strength of his legs.

His head swam, his senses whirling as he struggled to hold his balance.

Shit.

He hated feeling out of control. Despised the unfamiliar weakness of his body. His father was a Gen One Breed, which meant Micah's blood was among the purest of his kind. Yet he rocked on his bare feet as if he were a human toddler just learning to stand.

Fury alone kept him upright.

Fury would carry him out of wherever he was now, and outside to hunt for a vein.

Once he'd fed, once his body had taken enough fresh red cells to heal itself, fury would keep him on the path toward justice for his fallen brethren.

He wasn't going to rest until he had it.

And he would let no one stand in his way.

CHAPTER 4

☾

"I'm still not sure this is a good idea." Dressed in a casual, cotton summer dress and flats, Phaedra set her small travel bag down in the grand foyer of the Order's Rome headquarters to greet her friend. "I've never been away from the shelter for as much as a day since I opened it."

"That's exactly the point." Sia arched a platinum brow before pulling Phaedra into a brief embrace. "This little break is long overdue."

Phaedra sighed, uncertain, as she met her fellow Atlantean's gaze. "Maybe I should rethink the whole idea. After all, I haven't been back to the colony in ages."

It was no exaggeration. The enclave of immortals who had defected from the larger realm of Atlantis millennia ago would always be her people, but it had been nearly a century since Phaedra had left their mist-shrouded island to make a new life for herself among the mortals in Rome.

During those many decades away from her Atlantean people, she had lived fully, loved deeply, and had lost more profoundly than she believed possible. Now, her life was devoted to helping others. All that mattered to her was trying to bring a bit of light to a fragile world that seemed eternally cursed by violence and self-destruction.

For the scores of terrified and abused women and children who'd sheltered in her home over the years, the food and safe haven she provided had often meant the difference between life and death. Sometimes, Phaedra's efforts weren't enough to save them. It was those rare few that haunted her sleep. The failures. The circumstances she had been powerless to change.

Her dreams were haunted with another face now, too.

She didn't even have to close her eyes to see the harsh handsomeness of the Breed warrior with the piercing lavender gaze.

He'd crowded her thoughts like a ghost for the past week. Despite that he wasn't real—that none of her awful nightmare existed anywhere but in those fitful, disturbing moments of her sleep—Phaedra still recalled the cold accusation in his deep voice when he realized she was Atlantean. She still felt the stunning heat from the blast of otherworldly light that had ignited without warning, incinerating everything in its reach.

She could still hear the anguished screams that ripped through the wasteland in the instant before she woke up.

She shook her head, more in an effort to chase away the terrible memories than anything else.

Not that it worked. So far, nothing had.

She didn't think a week at the colony would be much help, either. Idle days on a mystical Mediterranean island would only give her more time to think. More time to relax, and possibly fall back into the dream she never wanted to visit again. She didn't need a vacation. What she really needed was to keep busy, like always.

Hesitating, she caught her lip between her teeth.

"This is a mistake, Sia. I should go back to the shelter—"

"The shelter will be just fine without you until you return. Trygg and I will see to that personally." Looping her arm around Phaedra's, Tamisia started guiding her farther into the mansion. "Anyway, you can't back out now. Zael and Brynne are already here, waiting to bring you to the colony with them."

As she spoke, Sia walked Phaedra to one of the large rooms off the foyer. The quiet rumble of conversation faded to a pause as they reached the entrance. Seated inside on sumptuous sofas and chairs were several members of the Rome command center she'd met through Sia and Trygg, along with Ekizael and Brynne, the mated couple who in recent months had taken on a diplomatic role between the Breed warriors of the Order and the Atlanteans of the colony.

Another Breed male sat with the group as well, someone Phaedra had never seen before. Tawny-haired and grim, he glanced at her in unreadable silence from across the room, his broad shoulders hunched forward as if he carried a heavy burden on his back, his big hands clasped together between his spread knees.

As she entered the room with Sia, all of the males rose, including the stranger. Her fellow Atlantean was the first to greet her. Zael's golden handsomeness and dazzling smile belied the fact that he had once served in the highest ranks of their queen's legion of deadly guards.

"Phaedra. It's been a long time. How good to see you again."

"You as well, Ekizael."

He reached out to the stunning brunette beside him and brought her closer. "This is my mate, Brynne."

"Hello, Phaedra." The tall beauty spoke with a refined British accent. "I've very much been looking forward to meeting you."

"Likewise," Phaedra said, returning Brynne's warm smile and greeting. "The pleasure is mine, Brynne."

Although this was their first face-to-face introduction, Phaedra was well aware of the daywalking Breed female who had captured Zael's seemingly untamable heart. That she was gorgeous came as no surprise, but there was also a keen intelligence and courage in Brynne's eyes.

As for Zael, he gazed at his mate with unmasked pride—and no wonder. Brynne had recently won the trust and respect of the entire colony when she helped defeat a traitor who had not only slain one of their council elders, but had also intended to steal an irreplaceable treasure—the colony's sacred, powerful crystal.

Without it, the hidden enclave would have no protection from the outside world, including the whims of their mercurial queen, Selene, whose reign over the larger Atlantean realm appeared to be growing increasingly desperate . . . and volatile.

"Tamisia told me about the trouble on the island a few months ago. The colony was very fortunate to have both of you on their side when Elyon's collusion with Selene was exposed."

Zael gave a grim nod. "All credit goes to Brynne, if you want to know the truth. Without her at my side, I wouldn't be standing here today and Elyon would've escaped back to the realm to trade the crystal for Selene's favor."

Lazaro Archer, the dark-haired commander of the Order's presence in Rome, gave a dry grunt. "Trading it to the Atlantean queen might've been the best-case scenario. Imagine if the traitor had decided there might be more profit in taking the crystal to Opus Nostrum."

Phaedra's skin prickled at the mention of the secret cabal whose escalating acts of terror had been making news around the world for months. The idea of a violent group like that obtaining the power of an Atlantean crystal made her blood run cold in her veins.

There were only five of the egg-sized, unearthly energy sources in existence, and no chance of there ever being any more. Phaedra felt that reality more personally than most. After all, her parents had been the ones responsible for creating the crystals long, long ago.

Brilliant scientists and alchemists, they had literally given their lives in devotion to their work. They'd been gone for many centuries, from the time Phaedra was just an infant, but she still felt their loss to this day.

"Who's to say Selene and Opus aren't working together?" The low-growled comment from the tawny-haired stranger drew everyone's attention. "Someone's pulling Opus's strings. We can't be sure it's not the Atlantean queen."

Lazaro let go of a quiet curse. "We'd better all pray to hell they're not. The Order's got its hands full enough lately putting out Opus's fires. If they were to join forces with a madwoman like Selene—"

"It would be all-out war." This time, it was Trygg who chimed in with a grave prediction.

Phaedra swallowed. Before the warriors had the chance to delve any deeper into Order business or the tactics of their violent trade, Tamisia pointedly cleared her throat.

"Please, forgive my manners. Phay, I don't think you've met Tegan."

"No, I haven't." The rest of the males halted their conversation, all of them staring at her now.

"Tegan, this is my dear friend, Phaedra." She offered a reassuring smile. "Tegan and his son will be flying back to the States with Zael and Brynne after they return from the colony."

He acknowledged her with a vague incline of his head and a perfunctory shake of her hand, as if he wasn't accustomed to social gatherings, or had no patience for being friendly. Something weighed heavily on him. Phaedra could see the burden of it in the hard lines of Tegan's beard-shadowed face.

It was hard to picture the hulking warrior as the father of a child, and she couldn't help but wonder what kind of son a menacing-looking Breed male like Tegan might produce.

Breaking away from his sharp gaze, she glanced to Zael and his mate. "Thank you for offering to escort me to the colony. I feel terrible for imposing on you and Brynne."

"I'm the one who should feel terrible," Sia cut in. "And I do. If I hadn't lost Phay's crystal amulet at the bottom of the Mediterranean, she'd be able to teleport to and from the colony—or anywhere else—anytime she wanted."

Phaedra shook her head. "Please, stop blaming yourself. I gave it to you willingly. Besides, if you hadn't been wearing the crystal, you wouldn't have been able to reach Trygg in time to save him. Seeing the two of you so happy together is well worth the amulet's loss."

Tamisia's gaze warmed as it lifted to meet Trygg's. The big warrior wrapped his muscled arm around her slender waist, drawing her against his side. If Tegan looked menacing, Trygg, with his shaved skull, scarred face and dark eyes bordered on monstrous. But there was a rugged handsomeness in his expression, especially when he was looking so smitten with Sia.

It had been a long time since a man had looked at Phaedra with such tender affection. Not so long, however, that she couldn't recognize true love when she witnessed it—between Trygg and Sia, as well as Zael and Brynne.

"It's an honor to escort you to the colony today," Zael said. "I'd be pleased to do so even you didn't need me just for my amulet. If you're ready, we can leave at any—"

The jarring sound of a piercing alarm went off somewhere inside the mansion.

Phaedra shot an anxious look at her friend. "What's happening?"

Lazaro Archer was the one who answered. "Someone tripped the security system down in the command center."

"Micah." The name was barely off Tegan's tongue before the temperature in the room went a little colder and the air shifted as with the coming of a storm.

The source of that disruption was making his way toward the foyer. Uneven, heavy footsteps slapped on the marble flooring. Labored breathing huffed and hissed, punctuated with a low groan unlike anything of this earth.

With Tegan rushing out of the room ahead of everyone else, the others followed, Phaedra included. She hung toward the back of the group as they all poured out, gripped in a mixture of apprehension and curiosity.

Between the bodies in front of her, she caught fleeting, obstructed glimpses of the obviously pained Breed male who had staggered up from the warriors' headquarters located below the mansion at ground level.

Even with his head slumped forward over his bare chest and broad shoulders hunched from obvious pain and weakness, there was no mistaking that he was easily as sizable as Tegan or Trygg. He prowled into the foyer like a wounded animal—and no less dangerous, Phaedra was certain. Menace rolled off him, along with an iron-willed determination that seemed to power him forward despite that he looked only a few steps away from death's door.

Tegan rushed to his side, catching the equally immense male under the arms and lending support just as his bare feet faltered and his knees began to buckle.

"It's all right, son. I've got you."

This was Tegan's son?

All her imaginings of him with a child went up in flames. His son was not a boy at all, but a full-grown, formidable man. Thick, tawny-brown hair in a soldier's cut crowned his head, choppy and bed-mussed. Smooth golden skin covered in Breed dermaglyphs, which pulsed with mesmerizing, dark colors. All he wore were loose gray sweatpants that clung indecently to his thick-muscled thighs and the unavoidably distracting area of his groin.

Phaedra was far from a blushing maiden, but the sight of his raw masculinity flooded her senses with an intense, uncomfortable awareness. Cheeks overheating, she glanced down, embarrassed to be ogling an injured man who was also clearly suffering.

She heard Tegan curse low under his breath. It sounded less angry than racked with concern. "You shouldn't be out of the infirmary, Micah. It's too soon. You need rest."

"Fuck that," came the deep, snarled reply. Micah's voice was all gravel, as if he hadn't used it for a year. "I need to . . . feed. Need to get out of here."

Phaedra glanced up again as Micah started to push forward. Tegan moved in front of him, blocking his path.

"Yes, you do need to feed. But you're not going anywhere. For one thing, it's morning beyond that door. For another, the only place you're going is back to D.C. with me."

"My team—"

"We've got a search unit going in tonight to find them. We'll comb every godforsaken corner of Siberia until we locate—"

"They're dead," Micah growled. "They're all fucking dead. I should be too."

He lifted his head then, and from over Tegan's shoulder, his gaze pierced through everyone and landed on Phaedra. He blinked once, dark lashes falling over the stormy lavender eyes that had haunted her for over a week.

Eyes she was certain would've haunted her forever if she wasn't staring into them right now.

She inhaled a stunned breath. "It's him."

At her almost soundless murmur, Tamisia glanced over. "Him, who?"

"Him," she whispered, backing away from the group and tugging Sia with her. "The Breed warrior in the forest wasteland."

"You mean, the one you dreamt about?"

Phaedra nodded, swallowing in disbelief. "I thought he was just part of the nightmare. I thought he was killed with the others in the dream, but Sia, it's him. He's real."

Faith, how could it be possible that he was standing in front of her now? How was any of this possible?

"You."

All the fine hairs at the back of Phaedra's neck rose at the guttural scrape of his voice. When she looked his way, she drew in a sharp breath at the fury she saw in his narrowed eyes. The lavender burned away in an instant, changing to a fiery amber that seared her from across the room.

All the hard angles and shadowed hollows of his face sharpened as he glowered at her. Behind the harsh line of his sneer, the points of his fangs erupted to fill his mouth.

He let out a dark, animal roar and surged forward, knocking Tegan out of the way as he charged for Phaedra. As he lunged, she leaped back, raising her hands in reflex. But she didn't need to summon her light to protect herself.

Snarling and gnashing his teeth, Micah was stopped only inches from her, halted by no less than three large Breed males and one former Atlantean soldier.

Even in his weakened state, it took all four of them to hold him back as he fumed and fought to get at her, his molten eyes trained on Phaedra in murderous rage.

"You," he seethed. "You were there."

Heart slamming against her rib cage, she shook her head. "No. That's impossible. It . . . you . . . none of this can be real."

"I saw you." The accusation boiled through his teeth and fangs as he bucked against the hands that restrained him from killing her where she stood. "I saw your glowing hands right before the explosion lit up the sky."

Tegan's green gaze sliced her way. "What's he talking about?"

"It . . . it was a dream." Phaedra shook her head again, feeling the weight of every pair of eyes locked on her now. "About a week ago, I had an awful nightmare—"

"She was there," Micah snarled, fire filling his irises. "The night my team was incinerated. I saw her. I spoke to her. Fucking Atlanteans. I should've taken you out when I had the chance."

He made another grab for her, practically dragging the other males with him. The burst of energy cost him, though.

His breath rolled heavily through his parted lips, sweat beading on his face and powerful chest. His chin sagged, all of his powerful muscles trembling with strain. One of his knees started to give out, but several pairs of arms kept him upright.

When Micah's body slumped into semiconsciousness, Tegan cursed. "Let's get him back down to the infirmary and get him fed while he can still drink on his own."

Lazaro Archer nodded. "I'll have a blood Host brought in at once."

"As for you," Tegan said, swiveling at hard look at Phaedra, "it sounds like you have some explaining to do."

"It was only a dream." She inclined her head. "I promise you, I have nothing to hide."

"You'd better hope not."

"She's telling the truth," Sia said, stepping forward with all the authority of her former status as an Atlantean council elder. "I was with Phaedra when she woke from her dream. I've never seen my friend so upset or distressed. In fact, she still hasn't fully recovered. That's why she's going away to the colony to rest for a little while."

"Not anymore, she's not." Tegan's clipped reply was an unmistakable command. With his arms under Micah to help keep the big warrior on his feet, he sent a glower at Phaedra. "You don't leave this property unless and until I say so."

CHAPTER 5

☾

Micah took one last, long pull from the blood Host's wrist before sweeping his tongue over the punctures to close and heal the human's skin.

Shuddering as the thin red cells coursed down his throat, he sagged back onto his infirmary bed and waited for the blood to start doing its work on his depleted body. His father and Lazaro Archer had caught him up to speed on how Tegan had found him in a nomad's tent on the Kazakhstan wilderness after nights of searching, and the coma that had slowed his metabolism just enough for him to cling to life until Lazaro had arranged for his medevac to Rome.

His outburst in the mansion's foyer a short while ago had cost him precious strength, but already the blood he'd taken from his Host was knitting him back together.

He could have drunk more. Christ, he needed the

nourishment and then some. But if he'd been allowed to take his fill right now, he might've drained the pleasant, yet forgettable, woman Lazaro had brought in from the city to feed him.

Eyes closed, he listened over the drum of his strengthening heart and bloodstream as the human accepted her payment, then slipped back into her coat and was escorted out of the room. Her footsteps faded up the corridor outside, accompanied by the heavier tread of the warrior who'd been tasked with returning her to the city.

"You scared the poor female half to death."

Micah lifted his eyelids and slid his gaze toward his father, who stood frowning at him beside the narrow cot. Groaning, he let out a slow breath, still waiting for his body to fully recalibrate. "I was as gentle with her wrist as I could manage."

Tegan shook his head. "Not the blood Host. Phaedra."

"The Atlantean?" Micah scoffed, recalling her startlement in the foyer. Unfortunately, he also recalled how soft and feminine she looked in her simple summer dress and delicate flats. "She ought to be scared. She's got to answer for the blood of five good men on her hands."

"We don't know that yet."

"Like hell we don't. She was there that night. It's not like I'd forget that face." Fuck, not even if he wanted to. Even before he saw her today, those wide, long-lashed golden eyes had been branded into his memory for good.

Not even the coma that had claimed him for the past week had been dark enough or deep enough to erase the vision of her delicate oval face, thick waves of glorious chestnut-brown hair, and ethereal, almost regal, beauty.

Sure, she was pretty, but that only made her more dangerous.

He pushed himself up to a sitting position, letting out a low curse as every cell and fiber in his body complained in protest. "I'm telling you, I saw her. I was close enough to touch her."

"I know what you said, son. And she says she wasn't there."

"Not physically, anyway," added Lazaro Archer.

The leader of the Rome command center and Tegan had waited alone with Micah as he fed. The pair of Order elders were still grim-faced and sober, but neither one seemed to share his mistrust of the female. Were the two seasoned warriors actually going to give the immortal's denial the benefit of the doubt?

Micah scowled. "I don't care if she was there in the flesh or projecting herself into those woods using some kind of Atlantean magic. She was the only one there besides me and my team in the instant before the whole damn sky lit up. That demands an explanation. Hell, it demands a full interrogation."

"Agreed," his father acknowledged gravely. "Now that you're back among the living, there are a lot of questions that need to be answered. Maybe we should start with the reason you and your team went AWOL after the mission in Budapest?"

Micah felt his jaw tense, a tendon jerking in his cheek. He glanced away from the shrewd, gem-green hold of his father's stare.

"That's what it was, am I right? Not missing in action, as we'd all been left to assume. You were absent without leave." When Micah glanced up, Tegan blew out a harsh breath. "Christ. It's true. Where did you go? What happened out there that night?"

"I fucked up."

As far as explanations went, it wasn't much, but it summed up the situation succinctly enough. Still, he knew he owed his father—and the Order—more than that.

Exhaling, he recounted his team's last movements. "We were on a covert assignment. For several weeks, we'd been surveilling the head of an emerging terror group that was stirring up trouble in the region. Real asshole. Seemed to get off on spilling as much innocent blood as he could."

"Igor Nagy." His father made the name sound like a curse. With good reason. It was rare that members of the Breed bothered with mass violence on their human neighbors, but every once in a while a sadistic piece of shit like Nagy decided to throw a grenade into the tentative, all too fragile, peace between man and Breed.

Under normal circumstances, it would be up to the Joint Urban Security Taskforce Initiative Squads to round up Nagy and his followers, but the wheels of JUSTIS moved too slowly for the Order's liking, and Nagy was proving to be more than a nuisance. Elusive, surprisingly well-funded, and apparently insatiable in his need for violence, the bastard had to go.

"He'd been next to impossible to track down, but our intel placed his hideout somewhere in the Siberian interior. We got the bastard, along with about a dozen of his soldiers."

"We're aware of the black ops mission to eliminate Nagy, and your team's success," Tegan said. "That's why you were chosen to lead the operation."

The flat statement of fact might have passed as praise from anyone else. Maybe it was. Either way, it should have felt welcome, coming from a warrior of his father's renown. Instead, it only made Micah's guilt weigh even heavier on his conscience. The men he'd served with, fought beside as brothers, deserved all the praise. Not him.

Not after he'd led some of the Order's finest warriors straight to their deaths in the middle of a godforsaken stretch of wasteland.

And for what?

A sense of déjà vu. A curious and compelling vision he'd been unable to shake or explain. Not to his team, and sure as hell not to his scowling father or the equally disapproving chief of the Rome command center.

"What I want to know is what happened after you and your men cleared that bunker," his father pressed. "Why didn't your unit report back to base per your orders from Commander Reichen?"

Micah cleared his throat. "Because I issued different orders to my men . . . sir."

The admission of insubordination was met with silence from the Order elders. They exchanged a grave look before Tegan's eyes cut back to him. "I hope you've got a damn good reason. Especially when you're the only one left standing. Barely, at that."

He had never lied to his parents, not once.

He'd never lied to the Order's leadership, either. As much as he might want to deny the stupid mistake that cost so heavily, he wasn't about to offer anything other than the truth now. If it meant the end of his time as a warrior, so be it. God knew, he deserved that and more.

"I don't have a good reason for taking my team

deeper into the interior that night. All I had was . . . a sense that I had to go in. I felt as if . . . as if something was pulling me forward, deeper into the taiga. The farther we went, the more barren the terrain became. The foliage disappeared. The trees were black, the ground like loose rubble under our boots."

"The Deadlands," his father confirmed, his voice low. "That might explain why your communication links abruptly went silent. About ten years ago, some kind of incident decimated a large swath of land in that region."

"Hundreds of thousands of acres," Lazaro interjected. "As I recall, there was a lot of finger-pointing, but no one has ever accepted responsibility or offered a full explanation for what happened. All we know for certain is that someone either fumbled or deliberately deployed a massive chemical weapon in the region."

"Possibly," Tegan said, his expression skeptical. He swung that dubious look back to his son. "What happened when you reached the Deadlands?"

"I led the team deeper into the black trees. I didn't know why. I didn't know what I was looking for, but I knew something waited for me. Then, I saw the white doe."

He stopped there, trying to decide how best to explain the most insane part of the story. Not that he should worry about that. The two commanders were already looking at him as if he'd lost his mind.

Tegan shook his head. "What white doe?"

"The one I'd been dreaming about for more than a week. Every time I slept, the same thing happened. The doe appeared and led me into a barren stretch of woods. It always ran ahead, just long enough for me to reach it, as if it wanted me to follow."

A dark look stormed in his father's eyes. "Are you telling me this dream is the reason you ignored mission procedure and a direct order from your commander to go trekking off on your own?"

Fuck. Although he spoke evenly, the incredulity and anger in that restrained tone were obvious. Micah understood it, but he was also fully cognizant of the fact that the two of them were cut from the same cloth. If the situation had been reversed and Tegan had felt the same inexplicable impulse to see what lurked in that forest wasteland, he wouldn't have waited around for anyone's blessing or permission, either.

Not that it excused Micah's actions. Especially when those actions had come at such a steep cost to his friends and comrades.

"This time, the doe wasn't a dream. It was real. And it wasn't alone. That Atlantean female upstairs in the mansion was in the charred forest along with it. She ran as soon as she saw me. At first, I was concerned about her being in that place alone. But once I caught up to her and saw her palms glowing with Atlantean fire . . . by then, it was too late. The forest erupted. The light was searing. I heard my teammates scream in agony in the distance behind me as the sky lit up with the heat of a hundred suns. Then everything went black."

His father said nothing, staring at him in a silence that seemed to roil with unspoken reactions. Shock. Confusion. Perhaps even a small measure of relief that his only son had been spared.

Disappointment in him as a fellow warrior, no doubt.

Micah had made a point all his life to excel in

whatever he undertook. He didn't make mistakes. He was never ruled by impulse or emotion, even to the point of machine-like coldness, according to the reputation he'd deservedly earned.

His instincts as a warrior had been flawless—until now.

"My God," Lazaro murmured in the quiet that hung in the room now. "What you're describing is nothing short of hell."

Micah couldn't deny that. Yet what he'd endured paled next to the fate of his team.

"I came to sometime later. My skin was blistered, peeling away in sheets with every movement. My throat felt scorched with fire. I could barely see through my burned eyes. All I knew was I needed to find my men," he said, pushing on with the rest of his report. "I dragged myself back to where they'd been before the blast, but I didn't see them anywhere. There was only ash and debris under me. It took a minute for the truth to settle in. My unit was gone. Somehow, I'd survived the worst of it, but what was left of my five teammates was scattered over the forest floor beneath me."

His father's measured silence didn't break as he listened. His stern face remained unreadable, utterly still except for the tendon that had begun to pulse along his jaw. When he finally spoke, his voice sounded wooden. "Do you have any idea how lucky you were?"

That toneless question held more emotion than the formidable warrior would ever express in words. Micah knew that. His father was Gen One, among the first generation of the Breed. Hardly the touchy-feely type, even if he wasn't centuries old and a full half blood-drinking, savage otherworlder.

Micah's mother was the only one Tegan permitted past his walls. There had been a time when Micah was a boy that he'd known some of that unguarded caring, too, but those years were long gone. The door seemed closed to him completely the day he'd announced his intention to follow in his father's footsteps and become a warrior.

"I don't know why I didn't die along with my team," he replied, shaking his head at the idea.

Why he'd been spared made no sense to him. Not only because he hadn't deserved to live when he'd been the one who led his men into that hellish attack, but because the intensity of the blast had been strong enough to incinerate five strong Breed males standing only a few hundred yards away from him.

Yet he'd survived.

He needed to know why.

And now that he was feeling his body coming back online thanks to the blood he'd consumed, he wasn't about to lie around in an infirmary for another minute. He needed to use every ounce of life in him to avenge his team and destroy whatever—or whoever—was responsible for the attack.

Pivoting on the mattress, he swung his bare feet to the cold tile floor. He stood up, prepared to take the first step toward the open door of the room.

"Where do you think you're going, son?"

"Back upstairs to get some answers out of the Atlantean woman."

His father gave a tight shake of his head. "I'll handle that. We're not finished here yet."

"As for Phaedra," Lazaro interjected, "I can personally vouch for her character. She's been a member of this community for decades and she's a close friend of Tamisia's."

Micah grunted. "There's another Atlantean female with blood on her hands."

"Sia's paid for her mistakes," Tegan said. "Since her exile from the colony several months ago, she's proven herself an ally of the Order time and again."

"Phaedra's never given any reason to doubt her," Lazaro added. "For her to have anything to do with the destruction you witnessed with your team, she'd have to be some kind of monster. For crissake, she runs a women's shelter out of her home in the city. Phaedra's a good, kind-hearted woman."

Tegan seemed to agree. "I sensed no enmity from her at all when we were introduced. If she were hiding something, she damn well wouldn't have been able to conceal it from me."

For what wasn't the first time, Micah wished he'd inherited his father's psychic ability to read another person's emotional state with a touch. An ESP talent like that would make his work for the Order a hell of a lot more efficient. To say nothing of how it would benefit him when it came to dealing with beautiful, possibly homicidal, Atlanteans.

Instead, like most Breed offspring, he'd been born with his Breedmate mother's unique extrasensory gift. If Phaedra had been human, Micah would have been able to telepathically hear all her sins and negative impulses.

Since he was denied that advantage, he'd have to settle for more primitive methods. Starting with an hour or ten of thorough interrogation.

He turned around to face his father. "Enemy or innocent, she was there with me in the Deadlands. I won't be satisfied until she gives me a damn good reason why."

From the infirmary room doorway behind him, he heard a quiet clearing of a female throat. Then Phaedra's soft, yet direct, voice answered.

"Actually, I believe I may have been there to find you."

CHAPTER 6

He rounded on her from where he stood with his back to the open doorway.

"So, now you do admit you were there."

The low, gravel-rough voice that had accused her of murder and worse upstairs in the foyer sounded less rusty now, but the deep growl had lost none of its menace.

Or its sharp bite of accusation.

He took a step toward her, his movement alone seeming to take some of the oxygen out of the room. Even half-dressed and without any weapons in his hands, this Breed male was formidable. Judging by the amber sparks glittering in his lavender eyes, his animosity for her hadn't cooled at all.

Phaedra felt Zael tense where he stood at her side. She'd persuaded him to bring her to the warriors' infirmary in spite of his advice against it. While the former Atlantean guard had been allied with the Order for some time, his readiness to protect one of his own practically radiated off him as Micah advanced.

"What do you mean you were there to find me? Who sent you?"

She shook her head. "No one."

Until she saw him in the foyer, alive and undeniably real, she had assumed her dream was merely a product of stress and long hours at the shelter, as Sia had suggested. But now she had to wonder. Atlanteans were a race full of empaths, telepaths, and other illuminators. Tapping into unseen energies and forces of light came as naturally as breathing to most of their kind.

Phaedra's parents, Maenos and Sindarah, were among the most powerfully gifted psychics the realm had ever known. With their passing, all those incredible talents were lost for good. She had inherited none of their gifts, nor her parents' shared obsession with science and alchemy.

Still, she wasn't without some Atlantean strengths. And she hadn't been living among humankind for so long that she didn't recognize the prickling of her immortal instincts.

"I believe I was meant to be in those woods with you that night," she said. "Whether to witness what occurred or to try to save you from it, I don't know."

A brittle scoff hissed through his full, sculpted lips. "Convenient."

"I'm telling you the truth. I have no reason to lie." Although his muscled body all but blocked her path into the room like a solid wall, she stepped forward anyway, refusing to let him think she could be intimidated. Even if she was, just a little. "As for whether I was there as we stand here now, flesh and bone, or on some other plane, I can't be sure. All I can tell you is it felt like a dream. Right before it turned into the worst kind of nightmare."

"Finally, something we agree on."

Zael cleared his throat. "Phaedra asked me to bring her down here out of concern for you, Micah. She wanted to make sure you were all right."

"Or maybe she wanted another chance to try to finish me off." Skeptical, those fire-tinged, pale purple eyes hadn't left her gaze for a second. "Keep your concern. As you can see, I'm alive. Unfortunately, that's more than I can say for my teammates. They're nothing but piles of fucking ashes now."

Phaedra had stood up to her fair share of rage-blinded men in her work at the shelter, but Micah's fury was something different. Not explosive and swift to burn out, but controlled and dark. His anger was pain-fueled and lethal, and it put a tremble deep in her marrow.

"I'm sorry about what happened to them, Micah. I truly am."

His face hardened at her sympathy. If he could have pushed her away from him physically, it wouldn't have been any more effective than the forbidding coldness of his expression.

"I'll ask you again, Atlantean. What did you mean you were in those woods to find me? How did you know my team and I would be there?"

"I didn't know. I was led there in my dream. A recurring dream I'd been having for about a week before that night." Phaedra paused, feeling the weight of Micah's scrutiny along with that of the other warriors in the room. "The dream never changed: I'm lost in a barren forest, alone. Just when I think I'll never find my way out of it, an animal appears on the path ahead of me as if it wants me to follow."

"What kind of animal?" The question rumbled out of Micah. The look on his face was challenging, but now edged with more curiosity than suspicion.

"A deer. It was a gentle white doe, the most beautiful creature I've ever seen."

Micah's clenched jaw tightened as she spoke. Although he remained unmoving, staring at her in unnerving silence, she didn't miss the subtle glance that passed between Tegan and Lazaro on the other side of the room.

Zael spoke up as he moved farther inside the room. "None of you seem surprised to hear this. What's going on?"

"That's what we need to figure out," Tegan said. He looked at Phaedra. "This white doe you saw in your dream—it led you to Micah and his unit?"

She shook her head, then shrugged faintly. "I didn't know she was bringing me to them, but now I think maybe she was. When I realized the doe and I weren't alone in the woods this time, that there were men there too, she vanished. That's when Micah spotted me. He had weapons on him, and he was dressed for war. He started chasing after me, driving me deeper into the trees."

"I wasn't going to hurt you, Atlantean," he muttered.

Phaedra met his glower. "Nor I you, warrior. Or your men. You can believe me or not, it's your choice."

"And you say you'd also been having this dream repeatedly?" Lazaro interjected.

She nodded, then felt some of the blood drain from her cheeks. "Also?"

Her attention had never fully left Micah, but now she felt the tug of something deeper than just an unwilling attraction when her eyes clashed with his again. "You've been dreaming about the white doe in the woods too?"

He inclined his head in grudging acknowledgment. "For a full week, every time I slept. It was the same dream over and over. I encountered the white doe in the Deadlands forest and it led me farther and farther into the labyrinth of skeletal trees. The sequence never altered. Not until you appeared."

"No. That can't be right." She drew in a breath, her pulse taking on a wilder tempo. "It's impossible."

It was one thing to suspect her dream had been some kind of premonition or a signal she was meant to follow. But this was something different.

That she and Micah might have shared the same recurring dream in identical detail went beyond coincidence. It was a sign of something much more than that. Something she refused to consider, let alone accept as truth.

Zael's quirked brows only made her discomfort double. "I've never heard of an Atlantean and one of the Breed sharing the Dreamscape before."

"That's because it doesn't happen. It can't." She turned her frown toward Micah. "You must be mistaken."

He seemed to take her denial as a personal affront. Arching a brow, he crossed his muscled arms over the bared, glyph-covered skin of his chest. "Are you calling me a liar?"

"No, it's just—"

"Just what? Now, what are you trying to hide?"

While she grappled with the very idea that she and this Breed male, this warring man, might share any kind of connection—psychic or otherwise—Zael stepped in to fill in the blanks for the rest of the room.

"The Dreamscape is sacred territory. To share it with someone else requires a rare bond, the rarest, in fact. A bond of the soul."

"Please," Micah scoffed. "It's not unusual for people to have similar dreams. Just last month, two of my teammates both had dreams they were rock stars with their own harems full of groupies. Their souls had nothing to do with that."

"Yes, people do have similar dreams from time to time," Zael said, sober where Micah had been dismissive. "But I'm not talking about people in general. I'm not even talking about the Breed. I'm talking about my people. Phaedra's and mine. And what you and she described was something more than just a similar dream. You didn't have the same dream about the white doe on separate occasions. It was identical, and you shared it at the same time. Not just once, either. The dream became reality. It brought you to the same place and the same moment in time through your connection in the Dreamscape."

Tegan's mouth had flattened into a troubled line while he absorbed what Zael was saying. "Are you talking about dreamwalking?"

"That's what it sounds like to me," Lazaro agreed. "Andreas Reichen's Breedmate has that ability. Claire can enter someone's dreams with them and walk around inside their unconscious mind. Is that what we're talking about here?"

Zael slanted Phaedra a meaningful look before he replied. "Not quite the same as that, no."

And wasn't that an understatement?

She couldn't keep her gaze from sliding back to Micah. He was a magnetic force, even when his mistrust and animosity pulsed off him in waves. He didn't appear enthused to be the subject of this discussion any more than she was.

He'd be even less enthused if he understood what their shared dream seemed to indicate.

"We saw the dream through one pair of eyes," she said, astonished to so much as think it, let alone put it into spoken words. "We experienced the dream together, Micah. As if we were one entity, the same being."

"The same soul," Zael helpfully added. "That kind of soul bond only exists between the most destined pairs of immortals. It's formed before birth, a destined connection. Fated mates."

"Bonded souls? Fated mates?" Micah let out a chuckle. "No offense, Zael, but save the Atlantean love-and-light bullshit for someone else."

Zael merely shrugged off the remark with his typical laid-back calm. Phaedra, however, rankled. The former legion guard didn't need her to defend him, but she couldn't stand by and listen as Micah denigrated one of the most sacrosanct bonds of an Atlantean's life as if it was some kind of crude joke.

Even if she herself suddenly wished she didn't believe it could be true.

"Our culture is not, as you call it, bullshit." Her sharp tone drew his attention her way. She couldn't read the look on his handsome face, but some of his bluster seemed to fade under her glare.

He cocked his head, studying her. "You don't actually buy into this, do you?"

"It's not a question of whether I do or not. The dream we shared was real. It led us to each other in those woods. It happened. Even you can't argue that. It can't be wished away, no matter how much both of us might like to."

"I'd like to wish away everything that happened over this past week," he said. "But I can't do that, either. I'm a soldier. I deal in facts. Hard truths. I deal in reality, even when it's ugly. What I don't deal in is mystical, metaphysical nonsense."

"Soul bonds are not nonsense," she shot back. "My own parents shared that kind of bond. It was nothing short of destiny and fate that brought them together."

He grunted, a harsh smile on his lips. "Fortunately for both of us, those are two more things I don't believe in."

Phaedra wanted to laugh at his naivety, but there was nothing humorous about any of this to her. It was bad enough that she had to defend herself against his accusations that she somehow had a hand in whatever killed his men and nearly took his life too. Now, she felt compelled to convince this man—this overbearing, arrogant Breed male—that the dream they shared meant they were destined by some higher purpose to find each other.

She nearly groaned at the weight of that thought.

All her life, she'd assumed the soul bond would elude her the same way her parents' extraordinary gifts had passed her by. She had never been more desperate to hold on to that belief.

Why now? Why him?

It didn't make sense. And if it was fate controlling their paths, she couldn't think of anything worse than being linked to a warrior.

She'd built her life outside Atlantis on caring for people, on keeping the peace no matter what it cost her.

Now this?

Closing her eyes for a moment, she brought her fingers to her temples where the sudden throbbing of her pulse was beginning to grow into a headache. Maybe if she went home and threw herself into her work at the shelter, she could forget about the dream, this man, and all the questions swirling in her mind.

"If there's nothing else you need from me, I'd like to go back to my house now."

The grave look on Tegan's face didn't give her much hope of that. "Actually, we're only getting started."

"What more can I tell you?"

"We still don't know enough about the attack on Micah and his men."

"I already told you, I had nothing to do with it."

Tegan gave her a nod. "I believe you, Phaedra. But you're the only witness to what happened. Anything you can tell us would be a help to the Order."

"Because we're going to find out the truth one way or another," Micah added in a low growl. "Whoever's responsible is going to pay for what they did. I mean to see to that personally."

She didn't doubt that for a moment. Micah may have been near death's door only hours ago, but he was healing now. The dangerous soldier she met in the scorched woods was a lethal force of nature now—much of it focused on her.

"I told you everything I know. If I could help you, I would."

As she held Micah's penetrating stare, she couldn't stop the horrific incident from replaying in her mind. The sudden blast of light. The visceral pulse of the energy that exploded all around them. She didn't know where the attack had come from or who had ignited it . . . but she recognized the unmistakable force of it.

She knew that power all the way into her marrow.

"What is it?" Tegan frowned, suspicion glinting in his eyes. He slowly shook his head. "You haven't told us everything, Phaedra."

He said it with such certainty it felt as if he could read her troubled thoughts. She didn't want to hide anything, especially when lives had been spent. Yet to voice what she was thinking might ultimately cost lives too. Innocent Atlantean lives.

She sent a nervous glance at Zael.

His brow creased with concern. "If you have information, you need to tell them. Tell all of us now, Phaedra."

She knew he was right. She looked at Micah, her chest tightening at the thought of the agony he must have endured. Astonished that he'd survived. Despite their clash, she couldn't deny her relief that he wasn't killed along with the others.

"The light didn't come from Atlantean hands. Not mine or anyone else's. It was too strong for that, too pure."

"Ultraviolet?" Lazaro asked, dread edging his deep voice.

She shook her head. As deadly as sunlight was to members of the Breed, what she felt in that barren forest was something beyond even that.

"There's only one source that can emit that kind of light and power." She looked at Zael again, seeing the grim understanding wash over his face. "It came from a crystal."

Tegan raked a hand over his head. "Holy hell. How can you be certain?"

"She is," Zael said. "Phaedra's probably the one person in all of the Atlantean realm who could tell you that without a shred of doubt."

"How so?"

"Because all five of the Atlantean crystals were created by her parents."

Everyone stared at her now, a mix of reactions playing across the three Breed males' faces. Surprise, curiosity, intrigue. All of those emotions churned like a storm in Micah's piercing gaze.

"Your parents created them?" he asked. "How?"

"They were alchemists and mystics. They were also soul bonded, which made their gifts doubly powerful. Using those combined gifts, they created an enormous energy source that provided nourishing light and impenetrable protection for our people."

Zael nodded in sober acknowledgment. "Without their work, Atlantis would've been vulnerable to every enemy. Even now, both the realm and the colony are shielded by their crystals. Our people owe Maenos and Sindarah a debt that can never be repaid. Peace be upon their souls."

Phaedra smiled sadly at his praise for them.

Micah frowned. "Your parents are dead?"

"For a very long time," she replied, still feeling their loss. "They gave their lives for their work with the crystals. The realm had five, but after losing the first two, Selene wanted more. Eventually, she pressed them to make a sixth. My parents didn't tell anyone that creating each crystal demanded some of their own inner light. The last one they attempted to create proved too much. There was an accident in their laboratory and they . . ." Phaedra glanced down for a moment. "They sacrificed everything for their work."

Tegan and Lazaro offered murmured condolences, but it was Micah's silent, lingering gaze that reached inside her and made the ache of loneliness feel even sharper.

When she didn't think she could bear the sensation any longer, he cleared his throat. "So, are you saying there could be a crystal out there in the Deadlands?"

"There has to be. That kind of blast couldn't have come from anything else."

He nodded tightly, and she could practically hear the wheels of his mind turning. He glanced at his father and Lazaro Archer. "We need that crystal. As soon as night falls, I'll head back out to the taiga to find it."

Tegan scowled. "Like hell you will."

"I'm healed. I know the way back to the area of the blast. I don't need a team behind me; I can run the recon on my own."

"And risk taking a second hit?" Tegan firmly shook his head. "You got lucky once. Don't think it'll happen again. Your ass is staying put until I decide you're ready to be back in the field, end of discussion. I'm not saying that as your father. I'm saying it as an Order commander."

Both males squared off against each other, evenly sized and obviously equally stubborn. "If there's another crystal out there somewhere, the Order needs to have it. You know it."

"Another crystal?" Phaedra couldn't keep from interrupting. Nor could she hide her confusion. "The crystals belong to Atlantis, to our people. What does the Order want with them?"

The warriors all exchanged a cryptic look, one that also included Zael.

She stared at the former Atlantean royal guard. "What is this really about?"

"It's a bit of a long story," Zael said, clearly hedging.

Tegan slanted her a contemplative look as well. "We'll tell you more on the way."

She frowned, not sure she liked the sound of that. "On the way to where?"

"Order headquarters in D.C. Based on everything I've just heard, Lucan Thorne is going to want to meet with you personally and ask a few questions." He stated it as if there was no room for further discussion or argument. "As you're already packed for a few days away from Rome, we can depart as soon as Lazaro arranges our flight back to the States."

CHAPTER 7

By the time the Order's private jet touched down in Washington, D.C., several hours later, Phaedra's head reeled with all of the astonishing things she'd been told during the flight. She couldn't decide which one shocked her the most.

To begin with, not only was one of Atlantis's original five crystals in the possession of Lucan Thorne and his Breed warriors, but it had come to them through the one-time captain of Selene's royal legion, a guard named Cassianus. This same guard who had fathered a child twenty-five years ago with Selene's daughter, Soraya.

The lovers had been doomed from the start, for everyone in Atlantis knew the queen's sole heir was demanded to remain pure. Cass and Soraya tried to defy that law, but their union ultimately ended in tragedy. After Soraya took her own immortal life, Cass fled

Atlantis along with his infant child—and one of the realm's remaining crystals. Knowing Selene and her legion would hunt endlessly for him and the two treasures he stole from her, Cass assumed a new life as a supposed mortal in Boston while carrying out a clever plan to conceal the crystal, and his full-blooded Atlantean child, virtually in plain sight.

Cass eventually paid with his life for crossing Selene. His daughter, Jordana, hadn't known anything of her father or her Atlantean origins until very recently. She had since taken one of the Order warriors as her mate, and while Phaedra hadn't heard the details of Jordana and Nathan's story, she didn't imagine it was an easy one.

As for Selene, her temper had long been legend. Betrayal was the worst offense, and she was not a woman to forgive easily. Or ever. The fury that had been poisoning her for most of her long life only seemed to have grown more bitter with these recent blows.

According to Tegan, Selene had all but declared herself at war with the Order and the entirety of the Breed.

Between the Atlantean queen's simmering ire and the frequent, escalating problems with a secretive international terror organization calling itself Opus Nostrum, it was clear the Order more than had its hands full in trying to maintain any kind of peace and stability in the world.

"You've been very quiet since we touched down," Brynne remarked. She sat beside Phaedra in the back of a large black SUV that had met their plane on the tarmac of a private runway at the airport.

Outside the dark-tinted windows, D.C.'s iconic buildings and monuments gleamed under the starlight as the vehicle sped into the heart of the city. Phaedra shivered under the wrap she'd pulled from her bag when they'd landed. She had been dressed and packed for a week in the sunny Mediterranean of the colony, not the bracing autumn chill of Washington.

"I had no idea of all the threats the Order was facing from all sides. You certainly have some powerful and dangerous adversaries."

"Now you understand why we need to hold every advantage possible," Tegan replied, seated beside Zael on the facing second-row bench.

Although there was plenty of room for everyone in the cabin of the spacious SUV, Micah opted to take the passenger seat next to the vehicle's dark-haired driver, a strikingly good-looking Breed male who'd introduced himself as Lucan Thorne's son, Darion. After doing his best to ignore her for the duration of the flight, Micah seemed equally determined to put as much space as possible between them now as well.

Not that Phaedra should notice, let alone care.

The less she had to cope with his simmering mistrust and prickly disposition, the better. To say nothing of the disturbing reminders of their shared dream and all the impossible implications that came with it.

"Having one of the Atlantean crystals certainly gives the Order an edge," she said, glancing at Zael in unspoken understanding.

He gave her a grim nod. "It's also one less crystal for Selene to wield against us, should she decide to escalate her contempt into an official war."

A low scoff sounded from the front seat of the vehicle. "I'd like to see her try."

Phaedra would have expected the comment to come from Micah, but instead it was Darion's deep voice that issued the challenge. In the rearview mirror, his dark brown eyes remained fixed on the highway ahead, but the glow from the dashboard lights illuminated the hard, determined set of his square jaw and firm, sculpted lips.

"Trust me, you would not want to see Selene's wrath up close," Zael replied gravely. "No one would want that. The only thing keeping her in check is the fact that she's got just one remaining crystal. She can't use it as a weapon without weakening its protective powers and leaving both herself and the realm vulnerable to any incoming threat."

"She would've had two, if the colony had lost theirs," Phaedra pointed out.

Zael nodded, but it was Brynne who answered. "That's why it's so crucial for us to continue fortifying our diplomatic strides with the council at the colony. They have to understand that while the Order will never take their crystal by force, there may come a time when we'll need the combined power of theirs and ours in order to hold off Selene."

"Or take her down," Micah growled from the passenger seat up front.

He and Darion exchanged a dangerous look, and for the first time in her life, Phaedra worried for her formidable, immortal queen.

Micah's grim statement hung over the silence in the vehicle as they navigated the city, heading onto a residential street lined with opulent embassy mansions flying a range of flags from various countries all around the world.

The SUV slowed in front of one of the largest estates on the row, a sprawling eighteenth-century compound set back several hundred yards from the soaring security gate at the street. No flags or signage declared the property to the public, but it was obvious the impressive mansion and grounds could be nothing less than the Order's global headquarters.

"Be it ever so humble," Darion quipped, pausing the vehicle for a retina scan at the entrance before continuing through the parting black iron gates and up the long drive toward the house.

They parked in an underground fleet garage the size of an airport hangar and lined with easily a dozen dark-windowed vehicles of varying makes and purposes. More than a few appeared to be outfitted for urban warfare, with chunky tires and sturdy chassis that looked as unstoppable as tanks.

Phaedra followed her escorts to an elevator, uncertain what to expect as the car rose through the building to the main level. If she'd envisioned the Order's headquarters to be a cold military bunker or a Gothic nightmare of black walls and lightless rooms, or furnishings crafted from the bones of Lucan Thorne's enemies, she couldn't have been more wrong.

Even more elegant and refined than the Rome command center's residence, the D.C. mansion was a feast for the eyes. Beautiful millwork, wood, marble and tile gleamed from every corner of the spacious living quarters. Stunning antique French and English furniture was complemented by lovely sculptures, paintings and tapestries. All of it was bathed in soft golden light from cut-crystal chandeliers and table lamps that glowed invitingly in nearly every room Phaedra could see. She hadn't been near such jaw-dropping luxury since she left Selene's court more than a century ago.

As dazzled as she was by the surroundings, it was nothing compared to her first glimpse of the people gathered to greet her as she stepped off the elevator with her companions. Three men and three women stood in the spacious marbled foyer, and there could be no mistaking the dark, commanding presence of the Order's founder and leader, Lucan Thorne.

Black-haired with stormy gray eyes, he stood at least a head taller than the other two Breed warriors accompanying him. One of them sported spiky, almost disheveled-looking blond hair and translucent silver-lensed sunglasses even though he was indoors. The other enormous male was dark-skinned and stoic, a wall of muscles and menacing presence that seemed at odds with the warmth in his brown eyes.

As for the women, Phaedra could hardly keep from staring. Each was a remarkable beauty, from the serene African American whose hand was linked with the blond warrior's, to the regal auburn-haired woman standing at Lucan's side. But it was the third female who captivated Phaedra the most.

Tall and athletic, with short brown hair and penetrating hazel eyes, it was her skin that held Phaedra entranced. It was covered in unusual markings—dermaglyphs. Phaedra didn't sense that she was Breed, but something about the woman put a strange prickle of "otherness" in her senses.

The female standing beside Lucan offered a polite smile. "You must be Phaedra. I'm Gabrielle Thorne."

"Hello." Phaedra didn't know if she'd be welcomed or treated with the same animosity and mistrust she'd received from Micah, but Gabrielle's kindness instantly set her at ease. So did the other two women who approached her with warm smiles.

"I'm Savannah," said the beauty with the mocha-rich skin tone and velvety voice. "The hot geek in the shades over there is Gideon, my mate."

"And I'm Jenna." Grinning at her friend's humor, the glyph-covered brunette strode forward. "I've been looking forward to meeting you ever since Brock told me you were coming."

Phaedra sent an acknowledging glance at the black warrior who beamed at Jenna as she spoke. "It's nice to meet all of you."

Lucan, who had been observing Phaedra with inscrutable silence, now gave her a slight nod. "I trust the flight was uneventful."

"Uneventful?" She let out a small laugh. "The trip was fine, but it's going to take me a while to process everything I learned on the way."

A faint smile tugged at the corner of his mouth, in spite of the gravity in his stare. "Zael personally assured me that you could be trusted with the information. He's never let the Order down yet. I expect he won't where you're concerned."

She heard Micah's low scoff from somewhere beside her. Lucan heard it too, of course. His gaze traveled the group, those thundercloud eyes managing to look both relieved and censuring at the same time when they landed on Micah. "Glad to see you on your feet again."

"Commander Thorne." His stance rigid with attention, he gave the Order's leader a deferential nod. "I wish the rest of my team could be standing here with me too."

Lucan grunted soberly. "We all do, son."

With a quiet exhalation, Gabrielle moved from her place at Lucan's side and drew Micah into a brief embrace. "We were all so worried about you." The big warrior stood unmoving until she released him, about as accepting of the affection as a giant oak tree. "Your poor mother has been beside herself ever since you left for Budapest a few months ago. All the waiting for word about you these past several days has been torture, especially for her."

Micah actually looked contrite at the mention of his mother's worry. His tawny brows knit. "Is she here?"

"She's on the way," Tegan answered. "Chase and his team in Boston will be picking Elise up in New York and bringing her with them."

"They should be arriving within the hour," Gideon added. His smooth voice contained the traces of an English accent. "Nathan and Jordana will also be making the trip."

Micah frowned at the news, raking a hand over his head. "I didn't expect to come back to a full-blown family reunion."

"Don't flatter yourself, brother." Darion chuckled as he gave Micah's shoulder a light punch. "They're all curious to meet Phaedra as much as they're coming out of concern for your sorry ass."

Phaedra's cheeks burned with the heat of the glower Micah sent in her direction. As friendly and inviting as everyone else was to her, his disapproval lingered. It burned. And although she might never succeed in convincing him she wasn't his enemy—that it was fate that dropped her into the barren forest with him and the white doe—there was a part of her that hoped she could persuade him to believe her.

After spending most of her life taking care of people, to earn Micah's unwarranted contempt for something as heinous as the attack that killed his comrades cut her deeply. It wounded her down to her soul.

She could probably blame that feeling on fate too.

As for the other persistent feeling that had put her senses on alert since her arrival moments ago, it hadn't let up for a second. Her instincts continued to buzz with the suspicion that Jenna wasn't quite human, but not Breed either, despite her visible dermaglyphs.

She had countless questions crowding her thoughts, but she couldn't bite back the one that rose to the tip of her tongue.

"I'm sorry, Jenna, I don't mean to stare. But I have to ask—what are you?"

"She's my amazing mate," Brock interjected, as he moved in close and wrapped his arm lovingly around his female. "That's the only definition I'll ever need."

Phaedra wished she could crawl into the floor. "Forgive me. I didn't mean to be rude."

Jenna smiled and shook her head. "You're not rude at all. I was born your basic garden-variety human, but some things . . . changed a while back." She paused, giving a nonchalant shrug. "Now, I'm sort of what you'd call a work-in-progress."

Micah smirked, gesturing toward her with a chin bob. "Seems like you've got a few more glyphs than you had when I left for Budapest earlier this year."

"Oh, yeah, a lot more." She glanced at Brock, her expression cryptic. "The dermaglyphs have been coming in fast and furious for about the past week now."

"So have the dreams," Brock said, a sober edge to his voice. "At the rate they've been coming, we'll need to expand the archive room to a full wing of the compound just to make space for all the new journals of notes you've been taking."

"Dreams?" Phaedra had swallowed at the mention, her curiosity piqued. "What kind of dreams are you having, Jenna?"

She could feel the weight of Micah's gaze on her even though she wasn't looking at him. His attention sizzled through her veins like an electrical charge. Was this strange sensation part of whatever bond their time in the Dreamscape had awakened in them?

Or was it simply her intense awareness of him as a man, that unwanted attraction she felt every time she looked at him or heard the low growl of his voice?

Either way, she was sure she didn't want to know.

"They feel like dreams when I'm seeing them," Jenna explained. "To be more accurate, though, they're memories. Very old ones. And they're not mine—at least, they shouldn't belong to me, yet they've become mine. The same way all these glyphs shouldn't belong to me, yet they do."

The explanation only raised more questions, but Phaedra figured she'd already pried more than she had a right to. Although Jenna seemed to be a frank and open type of person, she was obviously dealing with something serious if it was not only changing her physical appearance but also invading her mind.

"If you start seeing a white deer in those visions, Jenna, do yourself a favor and kill the fucking thing," Micah drawled. "If you don't, you'll wish you had. Trust me on that."

Outraged, Phaedra swung an offended look at him. "Is everything a source of mockery for you?"

"No. In fact, I'm deadly serious about most things." His lavender eyes pierced her, just as they had back in the barren woodland of her dream that wasn't a dream. Phaedra wanted to look away, but his gaze held her in an unyielding grasp, as if they were the only two people in the room. "If I had known what would happen if I followed that animal into the Deadlands, I would have strangled it with my bare hands. I damn well should have. Maybe then my team would still be alive."

Phaedra slowly shook her head, horrified at the violence in him. To say nothing of his disregard for destiny or things that were far bigger and beyond the grasp of anyone or anything that existed on the temporal plane.

"How do you know your men weren't going to die that night regardless of whether you followed the doe into those woods that night?"

"How do I know?" A bitter smile curved his lips. "Because I'm still here, and that's not how it's supposed to be. I was their captain, their leader. I was their friend." His deep voice lowered to nearly a whisper. "I belong with them."

There was a rawness to the words, punctuated by the flash of amber sparking in his irises.

Phaedra knew the Breed wore their deepest emotions in their changeable eyes, and in their dermaglyphs. Micah's skin markings were covered by the all-black patrol gear he'd worn when he emerged from the Order's infirmary in Rome. Still, she could see them in her mind's eye as if they had been seared there from the first moment she glimpsed him in person, half-dressed and wild with blood hunger, pain, and rage.

Only the slightest hint of a glyph peeked out above the neckline of his shirt. The arcing tendril snaked up the side of his strong throat, pulsing from bronze to indigo to black as he stared at her in silent accusation.

Jenna's voice broke the heavy quiet. "When Tegan called in from Rome, he said the two of you had been having the same recurring dream every night for a week before the incident in the Deadlands. I'd like to hear more about that."

"So would I," Lucan said. "Micah, I'll start with you. Darion will get you settled, then both of you report to the war room in ten minutes."

Micah gave a curt nod of compliance, then Lucan turned to Phaedra. "Gabrielle prepared a guest room for you. I'll send someone for you when I'm ready to hear your side of the situation."

Without waiting for her agreement, the Order's leader turned to Tegan. "We need to bring you up to date on some recent Rogue activity since you left to find Micah."

"Rogues? Just what we don't fucking need."

On a low growl, he fell in beside the Order's leader, who gestured for Gideon, Brock, and Zael to join them.

Micah's gaze lingered on Phaedra for a moment before he, too, stalked off in the other direction, with Darion at his side.

"Phaedra, this way," Gabrielle said, her voice a bright contrast to her intimidating mate's commands. "I'm sure you'd like to relax for a while. Let's take your bag to your room and then we can all have something to eat."

"Thank you," she replied, although comfort and her empty stomach were of little concern to her.

As she watched Micah disappear down a long corridor, she couldn't help thinking fate had made a colossal mistake dropping her into the Dreamscape with him. She might not be able to deny the dream that brought them together, but she refused to imagine that destiny could have inextricably tied any part of her to a snarling, violent-minded Breed warrior like him.

Forcing a smile she didn't truly feel, she followed the trio of women to the opposite end of the mansion.

CHAPTER 8

☾

When Lucan said he'd send someone for Phaedra once he was ready for her in the war room, Micah hadn't anticipated that he would be the gopher dispatched to retrieve her.

After rehashing the details of his leadership fuck-up and reliving the loss of his entire team, all he wanted was to hit the headquarters' weapons room and work off some of his self-directed aggression for an hour or ten. Instead, he found himself cutting an irritated path through the white-marble corridors of the mansion toward the guest room where he'd been informed Phaedra was resting.

The door to the large suite was open. At some point since he last saw her, she had changed out of the lightweight summer dress she wore on the flight from

Rome. Now, she sat on the edge of the king-size bed with her back to the room's entrance, wearing a wine-colored tunic and dark jeans. Her rich, long hair fell in a loose twist down the center of her spine, the curling ends brushing the top of the dove-gray duvet beneath her.

Her soothing voice was soft with affection as she spoke into the phone she held to her ear. "Please, don't worry about me. I'm sure I'll be fine. Yes, all right. I will. I can't thank you enough for all you're doing—"

Sensing him, no doubt, she swiveled her head and her gaze collided with his over her shoulder. "I'm sorry," she murmured hastily into the device. "I'll have to call you back."

Micah said nothing, merely stood at the threshold of the room, leaning casually against the jamb as she severed the connection and placed the phone on the bed.

Her golden eyes narrowed, she stood up to face him. "Do you always intrude on other people's private conversations?"

"If you meant it to be private, you should've shut the door."

Her pretty mouth twisted with obvious doubt. "Somehow, I don't think that would've mattered. Besides, I have nothing to hide from you or anyone else."

"So you've insisted."

"It's the truth."

He grunted, not yet ready to admit he was starting to believe her. "Who were you talking to?"

She folded her arms over her breasts, which only drew his attention even more to the perfect swells hidden beneath the soft fabric of her tunic. "If you must know, I was talking to Tamisia. She and Trygg are looking after things at my house while I'm away."

"You mean the shelter you run from there." At her suspicious reaction, he shrugged, stepping into the room. "Zael mentioned your work with women and children in need. How long have you been doing it?"

"For a while."

Something cryptic flickered in her eyes. There was sorrow there as well. Micah wasn't accustomed to looking for tender emotions in others. God knew he did his damnedest to deny any softness inside himself too.

It was how he excelled as a warrior in the handful of years he'd been a full member of the Order. Ruthless training. Zero mercy. No exceptions.

If he was curious about Phaedra's past, he told himself it was for the benefit of his vow to avenge his fallen comrades. She was still a question to be answered, nothing more.

"How long have you been away from Atlantis, Phaedra?"

She tilted her head. "I stopped counting a long time ago."

"Years, then." He stepped closer. "More than a decade?"

She exhaled a humorless laugh. "Many of them. Close to a hundred decades by now, I imagine."

Holy shit. The answer took him aback. Despite the knowledge that Atlanteans outwardly aged as slowly as the Breed, it still shocked him to think she could be any older than the twenty-odd years that showed in her luminous, unlined face.

Somehow, she seemed more than youthful as she studied his reaction. Standing in the middle of the big suite, thousands of miles away from her home and everyone she cared for, she seemed vulnerable and alone. The realization sparked a protectiveness in him toward her that he didn't want to acknowledge.

He couldn't acknowledge it.

Every survival instinct in him warned to hold the wall, to not allow himself to see Phaedra as anything more than a potential crack in the Order's security. Equally troubling, she was a distraction he sure as hell didn't need.

Not now. He wouldn't let her be, no matter what she or Zael believed about the dream he shared with her and the ludicrous idea that it might signify some kind of cosmic bond they were meant to feel toward each other.

Where the Dreamscape and Atlantean soul bonds were concerned, Micah felt nothing but doubt and disbelief.

As for what he felt for Phaedra, he'd only be lying to himself if he didn't own up to the fact that she was the most breathtakingly beautiful female he'd ever seen. Desire licked through his veins as he watched her move to where her open travel bag sat. She picked up the light shawl she'd been wearing earlier, her hands graceful as she idly folded it and placed it on top of the rest of her clothing.

"I lived at the colony for most of that time," she said after a moment, her voice quiet and contemplative. "Eventually, though, I made the decision to leave and start a new life in Rome. Time passed. Things . . . happened. One night I found a bruised, starving young mother and her small child huddled at my doorstep to wait out a heavy rainstorm. I invited them in, fed them, and offered them one of the rooms to sleep until morning. Not long afterward, I opened my house as a shelter for any woman or child who needed a safe place to lay their head."

He listened, struck by her courage, and her selflessness. Few would be so generous, not only with their home, but with their heart. "It's an admirable cause, Phaedra."

Although he had meant the comment sincerely, she didn't seem to take it that way.

She slanted a frown at him. "I didn't do it for admiration, or as some noble cause. It's a necessity. With so much ugliness and violence in this mortal world, the protection my home provides is often the only thing standing between these women and children and death—whether that's from neglect, or at the hands of someone they believed they could trust."

The emotion in her voice was palpable. As was the ferocity of her commitment to the people she was helping. It stoked a conflict inside him, both as a warrior and a man.

He approached her, watching her expression go from defensive to cautious to confused.

"I'm well aware of the rot in this world too, Phaedra."

"You mean because of your work with the Order?"

He lifted his shoulder, a vague confirmation. "Yes, because of that. But also because I have my mother's extrasensory ability for reading human sin. When I'm out among mankind, in close contact with humans, I hear it all. All their negative thoughts and darkest secrets. All their vices. Every twisted, sadistic pleasure they've either taken or craved."

She stared at him in a strange silence, studying him. An unbearable tenderness moved into her expression. "No wonder your eyes look so bleak sometimes. You've known enough hideousness and violence for a thousand lifetimes of your own."

Without warning, she reached up to his face. Her fingertips lit softly on the edge of his clenched jaw. Her touch seared him, even that fleeting, infinitely gentle caress.

His fangs punched out of his gums, blood hunger still a beast on a threadbare tether inside him since his recent recovery. But it was the other hunger that gnashed to be let loose.

Need, raw and dangerous.

It coursed through him like fuel racing to meet with flame. A low, possessive throb pounded in his pulse points as he stared at Phaedra, unable to hide the embers sparking in his eyes.

As much as he wanted to cling to his mistrust of who she was—of what she was—what he wanted even more was simply . . . her.

Fuck.

Not going to happen.

Mentally, he squeezed his fist around the desire that ignited inside him. With countless women in this city and all the others he'd stormed through during his missions with the Order, this was one he refused to crave.

Fate be damned.

Hell, maybe he was too.

He drew back, pushing out a rough scoff. "Violence is what I do, Phaedra. I'm good at it—some have said I'm the best."

Her smile was sad with understanding. "I don't doubt that for a moment."

"Good," he growled. "So don't make the mistake of thinking I need anyone's pity. And don't look for me to make apologies for what I am."

"No, of course I won't do that. I don't suppose there's much you'd apologize for. Perhaps nothing at all."

He ground his molars together, telling himself her anger was better than the gentleness that might undo him if he wasn't careful. He had an unfinished mission to complete. A promise he'd made over the ashes of his brothers-in-arms.

That commitment began and ended with the bolt of unearthly fire unleashed on him and his comrades that awful night in the Deadlands.

"Lucan's ready for you in the war room," he said, delivering the statement as crisply as a command. "And Phaedra, be warned. The deaths of my teammates will not go unmet. Not by the Order. Not by me. I will do whatever it takes, cut down any obstacle that stands in the way of my vengeance."

She swallowed, but instead of being cowed by his threat, her proud chin lifted. "If you're expecting me to condone war on my people, there's nothing more for us to say here."

Micah leaned in close, fewer than a handful of inches between their faces. "Any obstacle, Phaedra."

She stared into his eyes for a breathless moment, then stepped past him to walk out of the room with her head and shoulders held as regally as a queen's.

CHAPTER 9

Phaedra wasn't sure how she managed to sit across from Micah at the long conference table in the Order's war room for more than an hour without letting her gaze stray to him even once.

During the length of her interrogation by Lucan Thorne, Tegan, Zael, and the other Order warriors assembled in the room, she recounted every detail of her recurring dream and the one that had ultimately landed her in the Deadlands with Micah. She answered the many questions that followed, not only from the Breed males scrutinizing her every word and expression, but also the inquiries from Jenna, Gabrielle, and Savannah.

Through it all, she held her head high and kept her eyes averted from the heat of Micah's unflinching stare.

Call it sheer determination to ignore him. Her stubborn streak had been honed over literally centuries of living. Call it outrage. Certainly, she was full enough of that after the bold threat he'd issued in her guest room—a warning she had no reason to doubt whatsoever.

She was willing to call it anything, except the awkward feeling that had clung to her from the moment she'd given in to the embarrassing impulse to touch his cheek and speak her thoughts aloud.

She couldn't take back that idiotic, clearly unwanted, compassion, no matter how much she wanted to. Nor could she pretend she didn't still feel sympathy for the awful gift he described.

Phaedra had seen the inhumanity of man up close more times than she cared to recall. But to walk through life as an open receiver of every sick and depraved thought that poisoned the air around him? She couldn't imagine how he didn't go mad with the burden of all that ugliness.

Evidently, her concerns for him were misplaced.

Not to mention unwelcome.

A lull fell over the room as the Order elders and their mates quietly considered everything she'd just told them. Phaedra folded her hands in her lap, eager to be dismissed and away from the scrutiny—particularly that of Micah.

More than anything, she just wanted to be free to go home where she belonged.

"I hope I've been of some help," she said, addressing the group as a whole. She glanced at Lucan. "Now that you've asked your questions, how soon might I be able to return to Rome?"

She felt, rather than saw, Micah's muscled frame tense in the chair across from her. "There's still one question you haven't answered. The most important one. Are you still loyal to your Atlantean queen?"

Given no other choice, she finally met his unsettling stare. "As I've already told you, I left the realm ages ago."

"That's not what I asked. Your parents served Selene as loyal subjects. So loyal, they were willing to die trying to carry out her wishes. What about you?"

His challenge drew the attention of everyone else now. Phaedra had willingly told them everything they wanted to know and then some. None of them had questioned her integrity or demanded she repudiate Selene in order to prove her good faith tonight.

"I don't serve Selene any more than I do you, or the Order. Everything that does matter to me is in Rome. So, unless the Order is prepared to call me their prisoner, I'd like to get back there."

At the head of the long table, Lucan exhaled a slow breath. "You're no one's prisoner, Phaedra. And this compound is no place for a civilian—Atlantean or otherwise. Zael and Brynne will accompany you back to Rome tomorrow. From there, they'll be continuing on to the colony for a diplomatic meeting with the council. If what happened in the Deadlands is a harbinger of troubles to come, it seems prudent that we reconfirm the colony's agreement to ally with us if and when we call on them."

The couple nodded in agreement. "We can still escort you to the colony if you like, Phaedra," Zael offered.

She shook her head. "I just want to go home."

Relief settled over her to think she'd be on her way tomorrow. The sooner she could put some distance between herself and her unwanted attraction to Micah, the better.

At the far end of the table, Jenna idly tapped her pen against a notebook laid open in front of her. She seemed distracted, her forehead pinched as the rapid tap-tap-tap-tap continued from the pen held between her glyph-covered fingers.

"I know that look," Brock said. "What is it, babe?"

"Maybe nothing. Except—"

"Except what?" Lucan asked, his own brows furrowing.

"This is the first in-person account we've ever gotten of the Deadlands." She shrugged, but something about it didn't seem as casual as she might have intended. "I'd love to take some detailed notes from Micah and Phaedra about the area, so I can add them to our archives."

"That's a good idea," Lucan agreed. "You three can get started on that as soon as we finish here. Chase should be arriving with the group from Boston any minute now, so unless anyone has something else to discuss, we can wrap things up."

The warriors and the trio of women seated around the table shook their heads. All except Brock, who had swiveled his chair toward his mate now, his dark gaze serious.

"Is everything all right, Jen?"

"Yes." She smiled, reaching for his big hand. "I'd tell you if it wasn't. Besides, you'd feel it in your blood. Everything's fine."

With his expression relaxing, if only by a degree, Jenna glanced at Phaedra. "My mate worries too much."

He grunted, turning his hand over so he could clasp her smaller one in an affectionate hold. "My mate thinks she's invincible."

Jenna smirked. "Well, if the biotech implant fits . . ."

Phaedra couldn't contain her curiosity. "I don't understand."

It was Lucan who answered. "Around twenty years ago, Jenna was taken captive by one of the Order's most dangerous enemies. Before we caught up to him, he'd brutalized her and left a piece of himself behind."

As if to demonstrate, Jenna pointed to the back of her neck. "State-of-the-art, alien technology. Enhanced strength. Adaptive cellular regeneration. Memories that play like a horror movie." She grinned at Brock. "But hey, look at the bright side, right? I'll never get a gray hair and I suppose the full-body glyphs are kind of badass."

"I'm glad you can joke about it," he growled. "I only wish I'd been the one to kill the Ancient son of a bitch."

Ancient. The term he used was an old one, though not unfamiliar, especially not to Phaedra or any of her kind. Ancients were the fathers of the Breed. Savage otherworlders. Blood-thirsty, ruthless conquerors. A raiding party of eight such predators had come to Earth millennia ago and spent centuries hunting down and slaughtering both humans and Atlanteans wherever they could.

Ultimately, they had delivered a catastrophic blow to Phaedra's people. After managing to get their hands on a pair of Atlantis's crystals, they used the combined power of both to destroy the realm's original island home, decimating the population and forcing Selene and the scant hundreds of survivors to flee to a new location where they remained to this day.

The terror of those dark days and nights happened so long ago, it had nearly faded into myth.

Much like the Ancients themselves.

But one thing didn't make sense. Phaedra tilted her head, confused by the recent timing of Jenna's ordeal. "According to everything I've heard, the Order killed all of their Ancient fathers back in mankind's Middle Ages."

Tegan slowly shook his head. "All but one."

"Not counting the two who reportedly died of UV exposure soon after their ship crashed on Earth," Lucan added.

"How did the one survive?" Phaedra asked, horrified to consider one of those monsters had been loose in the world until just two decades ago.

"Someone hid him away until he was ready to make use of him," Gideon answered grimly.

Brynne scoffed. "Someone every bit as dangerous and savage as any of the Ancients. I ought to know. I'm a product of both of them."

Lucan grunted. "You're one of the few good things to come out of Dragos's twisted laboratory experiments, Brynne. You and your sister, Tavia, both. Strange as it is, we also have him to thank for some of the Hunters who've either joined our ranks or proven themselves to be trustworthy allies."

Phaedra sat back in her chair, overwhelmed with all of this new information—not to mention dozens of new questions she was dying to ask.

Before she had the chance to sort her thoughts, the sound of voices carried from the corridor outside the open war room. Everyone at the table rose as a big blond Breed male led a group of three warriors and three women inside.

A dozen conversations bubbled at the same time as the new arrivals were welcomed. It seemed like a happy reunion, even though an undercurrent of seriousness seemed to run through the handshakes and brotherly embraces of the men.

Phaedra hung back, feeling like the awkward outsider as smiles and friendly greetings were exchanged and the din of conversation filled the room.

Micah stood at the periphery of the crowd, too, though not for long.

A petite blonde who'd been caught in Tegan's strong arms from the instant she arrived now broke away and burst through the crowd to race toward Micah. "Oh, thank God!" she exclaimed, her voice choked with emotion as she captured him in a tight hold.

"Mom," he said quietly, encircling her tiny frame in his muscled embrace. "It's okay," he reassured her as she wept against his broad chest. "Everything's okay. Ah, Christ. Please, don't cry."

"I was so afraid I lost you." She drew back, eyes the same lavender color as his welled with tears. She held them back, tipping her head up to look at her son's stern face. "I don't want you leaving ever again, Micah. Promise me."

"I wish I could." His deep voice was as gentle as Phaedra had ever heard it. "You know I can't make you that promise, Mom."

"She knows," Tegan said, joining them now. "Don't you, Elise?"

He wrapped his arm around her shoulders and drew her close. She leaned into him, nodding shakily. "You two are everything to me. I can't bear the thought of ever losing either of you."

"You won't," father and son said at the same time.

There was so much similarity between them. But some of Tegan's hard exterior smoothed away now that he was close to his pretty mate. Seeing the love between them made a tightness bloom in Phaedra's breast.

The sense of loneliness took her by surprise. So did the sudden awareness that Micah was staring at her, his piercing gaze unblinking. Far too knowing.

Why must she always feel such a jolt whenever this male looked at her? If it was a mistake of fate that put them into the Dreamscape together, she only hoped she'd be able to purge him from her thoughts once she returned home to Rome.

Tomorrow couldn't come soon enough.

Eager for a distraction from their unsettling eye contact and the tender family reunion she had no business eavesdropping on, she turned her head. At the same time, one of the Breed warriors strode toward her with an ethereal platinum-blonde female at his side.

Phaedra knew instantly that she was looking at a fellow Atlantean. The woman understood the same thing, her smile beamed as she approached.

"Hello," she said, her warm gaze sparkling like the sea. "You must be Phaedra."

"Yes. And you, of course, are Jordana." Phaedra barely resisted the impulse to sink into a bow before Selene's granddaughter, the only living heir to the Atlantean throne. Mesmerized, she couldn't keep herself from staring. "You look so much like both your parents.

You have Cassianus's fair hair, but your beauty is all your mother, Soraya's."

Jordana inhaled a shallow breath. "You knew them?"

"Yes, I did. A long time ago."

"Oh." The young woman linked hands with the ebony-haired male at her side, as if she needed the grounding. When she spoke, there was a quiet wonderment in her voice. "I would love to hear about them, Phaedra. If it would be all right with you, that is."

"It would be my pleasure. I'll tell you whatever you'd like to know."

"Thank you," Jordana whispered, pressing her lips together. "I'm sorry, I haven't introduced my mate. This is Nathan."

"Nice to meet you," Phaedra said.

"Likewise." He was strikingly handsome, a study in black from his leather combat gear and boots, to his glossy, short hair. No doubt he was deadly, but there was no denying the tender feeling in his gaze when he looked at Jordana.

"Hey, is this a private party over here, or can anyone crash?" The whiskey-smooth drawl came from another of the warriors who'd just arrived. He walked with an easy swagger, and grinned with all the charm of a good-looking man accustomed to getting whatever he wanted. "I'm Eli."

"Phaedra," she replied, finding it impossible not to return the warrior's megawatt smile.

He gestured to the last of the Breed males who'd come in with the group and was now heading over with Darion Thorne. "That's Jax. He's far less interesting than me."

Athletically built and almost too beautiful for a man with his almond-shaped eyes and a curtain of sleek black hair falling around his shoulders and down his back, Jax prowled toward their little group with the grace of a cat. He wore the same black combat gear and weapons as his comrades, but slung across his muscular body was a leather strap bristling with razor-sharp throwing stars.

"Don't judge the rest of us based on this asshole," Jax said, winking at Phaedra as he jabbed an elbow into Eli's side. "We just keep him around for laughs."

Phaedra smiled. "Hi, Jax."

"Pleasure," he replied, with a small bow of his head.

They all talked for a few minutes, then Gabrielle came over and offered to introduce Phaedra to the people she had yet to meet. First was Sterling Chase, the leader of the Order's Boston command center, and his mate, Tavia, who was also the half-sister to Brynne. Then came Micah's mother and Tegan's mate, Elise.

"It's very nice to meet you all," Phaedra said, finding the group of them to be unexpectedly hospitable to the stranger in their midst.

All except Micah, that was.

He hung back while his mother clasped Phaedra's hand in greeting. "Tegan's told me what happened with you and Micah. The dream, the Deadlands . . . all of it." She glanced behind her to Micah for a moment, then brought her soft lavender eyes back to Phaedra again. "I don't know how it was that you ended up in those woods with my son. All I do know is, he's alive. If your being there that night has anything to do with bringing him home, then you will always have my gratitude, Phaedra."

The low rumble of Micah's voice dropped like a hammer on the tender exchange. "If we still have to meet with Jenna tonight, we should get to it."

The gruff comment turned Jenna's head away from the conversation she was having with Savannah and Brock. "I'm ready whenever the two of you want to get started. We can meet up in the archive room."

Micah gave her a curt nod. "All right. Let's get this over with."

He pivoted away and stalked out the door. His exit prompted the rest of the gathering to start breaking up too.

As the warriors and their mates began filing out of the war room, Jordana came up behind Phaedra. "I'd love to talk with you some more. I have so many things I'd like to ask you."

"Why don't you join us?" Jenna suggested. "I was just about to take Phaedra for a visit to Cyborg Central."

Jordana smiled. "You haven't seen Jenna's archives yet?"

"Uh, no I haven't."

"Then prepare to be amazed."

CHAPTER 10

As a boy, Micah had known only a passing interest in the headquarters' chamber reserved for Jenna's work. When he visited the Order's D.C. compound with his parents, he'd always been far more intrigued with the weapons room than the floor-to-ceiling bookcases housing the journals Jenna had begun using to record the history and culture of the Ancients, as shown to her by the alien DNA-infused implant embedded inside her body.

Firearms, throwing stars, explosives.

A gleaming blade crafted of Rogue-killing titanium.

Those were his passions.

Leave it to others, like Darion, to straddle the line between scholar and soldier with equal skill. Micah's expertise had led him down a single path, and he was damn good at what he did. He didn't need anything but the feel of a weapon in his hand and the knowledge that his dark work made the world a better place for everyone else.

Still, as he stepped inside the large room that had been Jenna's personal workspace for the past two decades, he couldn't help but be impressed.

She'd been busy since he'd last seen the place.

Leather-bound journals lined nearly every inch of shelf space now. Meticulous hand-drawn sketches, complicated diagrams, and indecipherable technical schematics had been affixed to the walls as if they were works of art. Hell, they practically were art, judging from the incredible level of detail she'd captured on them.

He strode over to one of the odd diagrams and was studying the tangle of linked formulas and sprawling flowcharts when several pairs of footsteps approached from the corridor.

Jenna entered first, her brows furrowing over her hazel eyes when she spied him looking at the sketch. "That one's unfinished. I've only recently started seeing visions of the design, but it feels . . . incomplete."

Micah gave a vague nod, curiosity making him peer a bit closer at the diagram. "It looks like some kind of operational sequence. A code of some sort."

"Think so?"

He shrugged, moving away from the sketch as Phaedra stepped into the room with Jordana.

"You didn't even say hello to me yet," Jordana lightly scolded him, walking over to give him a warm hug. Her expression softened as she pulled back and looked at him. "It's really good to see you, Micah. I'm so sorry about what happened to your team."

His face hardened at the reminder. Guilt and grief still clawed at him, but he clamped the lid down on all of it. "Still working at the art museum?"

"I am. Carys too, from time to time."

Micah had been introduced to Jordana by Carys Chase a few years ago in Boston, before Jordana had hooked up with Nathan and before anyone had reason to suspect that Carys's best friend had not been born a Breedmate, but a full-blooded Atlantean. A fucking Atlantean princess, no less.

Now, it seemed she'd found a fast friend in Phaedra.

Not that Jordana was alone in that. Everyone at the compound seemed willing to accept Phaedra into their confidence, even his own mother and father.

So, why was he finding it so damn hard to trust her?

Part of the reason was the five ash piles he'd been forced to leave behind in the Deadlands. But he was starting to wonder if the bigger reason he didn't want to let his guard down had everything to do with him. With the way she made his blood race with hunger unlike any he'd known before.

He wanted her, more than he was willing to admit. And that was a distraction he didn't need and sure as hell couldn't afford.

Not when he was fully prepared to go to war with her people if the attack on him and his unit traced back to Selene.

Would Phaedra stand in the way of that? He'd already vowed to run through her if she tried. He'd meant it. He only hoped she wouldn't put him to the test.

While he listened to Jordana talk animatedly about her newest acquisition at the museum, Micah's attention was rooted on Phaedra. She drifted farther into the archive room, her face lit up with astonishment as she stared at the hundreds and hundreds of volumes in Jenna's collection.

"These are all your writings?"

Jenna nodded. "I started with one journal, thinking I might be able to make sense of the visions I was having if I wrote them down. I never expected there'd be enough to fill one book, let alone all of these. And the visions are still coming. Lately, I've been filling about a journal a day."

"What kind of visions are they?" Phaedra asked.

"Sometimes I see vicious battles the Ancients waged throughout the centuries. Other times, I see wholesale slaughters of entire populations. Those are the worst things I've seen." Jenna let out a slow breath. "Now and then, I also see glimpses of life on the dark planet they came from, or strange things like those diagrams and memory snapshots of alien technology and equipment."

A small frown creased Phaedra's brow as Jenna spoke. Although she listened with obvious interest, Micah detected a subtle change in her. She seemed on edge somehow, anxious, the longer she remained in the room.

"What's wrong?" he asked, his voice drawing her attention.

"I feel—" She hesitated, giving a faint shake of her head. Her gaze flicked away from him, back to Jenna. "There's a crystal here. It's close. I can feel it."

Although the Order had been in possession of one of the Atlantean crystals for some time, Micah had been away training and on missions with his team the whole time. He had never personally seen the crystal Jordana's father had taken from the realm, or been anywhere near it.

He didn't have to ask Jenna to confirm Phaedra's suspicion. Her reaction was convincing enough. She glanced at him, her pale gold eyes wide, a full-body shiver making her tremble.

A storm of emotions played over her beautiful face, but underneath them all was an unmistakable look of heartache.

God help him, there was a part of him that wanted to close the distance between them and draw her into his arms. He'd barely stamped down the impulse before Jordana's alarmed voice brought him back to his senses.

"Um, Jenna?" She pointed past Micah's shoulder, to the far end of the long chamber where a hulking, large black floor safe stood. "You need to see this."

Jenna hurried over to look and drew in a breath. "Holy shit."

Phaedra let out a soft gasp when she saw it, too, her hand coming up to her parted lips.

Even Micah could only stare in astonishment.

A silvery glow surrounded the huge safe. The light pulsed with intensity, growing brighter with each passing second.

Jenna faced them, astonishment in her voice. "This has never happened before. Jordana's been in this room before. Zael too. I've never seen anything like this."

Jordana nodded in agreement. "I don't understand. Inside that safe, the crystal is housed within a titanium box. It's supposed to keep the energy muted. That's how my father was able to conceal the crystal from any of our people. How is this possible?"

"My parents," Phaedra whispered. "They're part of all five crystals. It's their life force I'm feeling. It's been so long since I've been in such close proximity to one of the crystals, I didn't remember how strongly I feel their presence."

Micah recalled her certainty about the presence of a crystal in the Deadlands. "Is this the same thing you felt the night my team was killed?"

"No." A strange, sad smile spread over her lovely face. "This is different. It's an overwhelming feeling of love, of light. That's what the crystals were meant to be. What I felt in the woods with you was something dark, a detonation meant to inflict mass harm."

"It sure as hell did that."

Phaedra swallowed, nodding soberly. "Each of the five crystals holds immense light and strength. They were created to protect, to provide power as a shield. The Ancients twisted that power when they annihilated Atlantis's original settlement. They manipulated the crystals, found a way to turn all that light and strength into a dark weapon. All it takes is the combined force of two crystals and the will to destroy."

The idea put a coldness in his blood—and iron in his resolve. Just another reason to make sure Selene never got her hands on more than the one crystal she had left.

And God forbid Opus Nostrum ever ended up with that kind of power.

While Micah's thoughts churned with all the disturbing scenarios that were possible, the locked door on the safe opened on its own, as if in invitation. Phaedra began to walk toward it.

A jolt of dread shot through him, images of the scorched carnage left behind in the Deadlands flashing in his head. He reached out, halting her, his hand clasped around her wrist. "Stop, Phaedra. You're not going anywhere near that thing."

She arched a brow. "If you're still concerned I'm secretly in league with Selene and that I might try to steal the crystal from right under your nose, you needn't worry. If that's what I wanted to do, I'd already be gone with it."

He growled under his breath. That wasn't the source of his concern at all, even if it should be. To his shock, the only concern he had right now was her.

Even though she wasn't a fragile human by any means, he didn't want to imagine what might happen if she was wrong. For all his mistrust and suspicion in the beginning, he had to admit some of those walls were coming down the more time he spent with her.

Pulling out of his loosened hold, she continued to approach the glowing safe. She paused in front of the opened door and looked back at Jenna. "Do you mind if I take it out?"

Jenna shook her head. "It belongs to you as much as it does anyone else."

As Phaedra reached inside to retrieve the small metal box, the glow surrounding the safe spread to her. Soft silver light skated over her limbs and into her hair, infusing her chestnut waves with unearthly luminescence.

She was stunning anytime, but bathed in the glow from the crystal, she was nothing less than a goddess kissed by heavenly fire. Micah stared. Christ, he could hardly do anything else as he watched her walk back to the group.

She set the small box down on the worktable in the center of the room as he, Jordana, and Jenna gathered around.

Jenna slid a hesitant look at him. "Since we haven't seen this kind of reaction from the crystal before, I'm not sure you should be here when we open the box."

"It's all right," Phaedra said. "This light will bring no harm to him."

Micah smirked. "You sure about that? You've probably got more than a few reasons to want to scorch my ass."

"Now that you mention it." She gave him a wry smile. "If you think you can trust me, stay."

Crossing his arms over his chest, he gave her a nod to continue.

She lifted the lid on the titanium box, then gingerly reached inside. The crystal was smaller than he'd expected—roughly the size of a hen's egg. But the power that emanated from it was indescribably intense.

The hairs on his arms prickled as Phaedra lifted the crystal out of the box and held it in her palms. His veins thrummed, his cells vibrating as he stared at the silvery, translucent orb that looked similar to mercury glass. The soft glow that clung to both the crystal and Phaedra warmed the entire room, not with cosmic fire as he'd experienced in the Deadlands, but with a peaceable, soothing calm.

"You can feel it, too," Phaedra said, less a question than a certainty.

He nodded. So did Jenna and Jordana.

"You feel them," she said. "That warmth you feel is my parents. This is the only way for me to be near them now, to touch them."

Phaedra's eyes closed and she held the crystal in silence for a short while, cradling it like a precious treasure. Her expression softened as if she could feel things beyond the others in the room. As if she were communicating in a wordless language with the small orb that glowed in her palms.

When she opened her eyes again, they glistened with emotion. The illumination that had surrounded her slowly faded, all of the light seeming to pour back into the crystal, where it swirled and sparked.

Gently, she placed it back inside the box and closed the lid.

"Thank you, Jenna," she said, her voice quiet.

As Jenna returned the box to the safe, Phaedra walked slowly out of the room. Micah followed, catching up to her in the corridor. Although her skin and hair were no longer infused with light, the calmness lingered. But so did a tender sadness.

"Are you okay?"

She met his gaze and gave him a small nod. "I miss them, that's all."

She lowered her head, and a tendril of her rich brown hair fell into her face. Before he could stop himself, Micah reached out and smoothed the lock behind her ear. Her silken hair glided through his fingers. This close to her, the scent of lemons and roses and something far sweeter than either one hit his nose like a drug, sending his pulse racing.

The heat of her skin radiated toward him, making him hot with the need to feel her curves crushed against his body. Against his will, he recalled her tender touch on his face earlier tonight. The memory made him burn all over again, made him want to feel her caress on more than just his cheek.

She looked up at him again, her lips parted as if she was about to say something. If there had been any hint of permission in her voice, he wouldn't be fool enough to reject her again. If she gave him even the slightest indication that she didn't think he was a complete bastard, he'd claim her mouth in a blazing kiss right where they stood.

Christ, he wasn't sure it would take even that much for him to act on his desire for her.

"Hey, Micah." Darion hailed him from the other end of the corridor. He was walking alongside Nathan, with Jax and Eli trailing behind.

Micah groaned at the interruption, but in his gut he knew he should be relieved. Phaedra took a step away from him as the four males strode up to them.

"We're all heading out to the city to catch up," Darion said. "We're going to hang out at Slake for a while. You want to join us?"

Micah was more than passingly familiar with the Georgetown blood Host parlor, and the fact that Darion kept a luxury VIP suite there. Over the years, Micah had partaken of the establishment's services more than a few times.

It had been several long hours since he fed back in Rome. His healing body sure as fuck could do with more sustenance, to say nothing of the other options available for purchase at the exclusive club that catered to the Breed.

Putting some distance between him and Phaedra wasn't a bad idea either.

At that moment, Jordana stepped out of the archive room. She sent a smoldering look at her mate, Nathan. "Did I hear someone mention Slake?"

Nathan's stern face broke into a rare smile. "This is becoming a habit every time we come to D.C., love."

"Are you complaining?" Jordana laughed as she walked into Nathan's embrace. "You're the one who's corrupted me."

Nathan stroked her cheek. "Baby, I'll never complain about making you happy."

"Good." She glanced at Phaedra. "You should come with all of us."

"What's Slake?"

"It's a feeding parlor," Micah growled, appalled at the idea of gentle, lovely Phaedra getting a firsthand glimpse of the baser natures of his kind. He turned his scowl in her direction. "You wouldn't like it."

"You don't know that," Eli interjected, a grin accompanying his whiskey-smooth drawl. "It's one of the swankiest clubs in Georgetown, Breed or otherwise."

Jax nodded. "It also has two dance floors and sim-lounge. You should come."

Micah felt his frown furrow deeper. "It's not Phaedra's kind of place. Trust me."

"Nathan didn't think it was my kind of place either," Jordana argued. "Besides, Phaedra and I haven't had a chance to talk yet, and she's going back to Rome tomorrow."

Why the reminder of her departure should put a twinge of regret in him, Micah didn't care to know. Her gaze met his and an unspoken acknowledgment of the desire still crackling between them made her golden eyes dusky with awareness.

"I should probably stay here," she said. "I'd love to spend some more time with you, Jordana, but Jenna wanted me to tell her more about the incident in the Deadlands before I have to leave with Zael and Brynne."

"I can wait," Jenna said, stepping out to join the small group in the corridor. "I'm actually feeling a little tired right now, anyway. If you don't mind, we can meet again tomorrow before you have to go."

Micah might have suspected it was only an excuse, but Jenna did look a bit piqued. "Is anything wrong?"

"No. Just par for the course lately. I'm just going to close my eyes for a while. You all have fun."

As Jenna headed for the elevator up to the mansion's residence, Jordana smiled. "I guess it's settled. Shall we go?"

"Tell you what," Eli added, turning all of his easy charm on Phaedra. "If you decide you don't like the place at any time after we get there, I'll personally see you back here to the command center."

"Like hell you will," Micah muttered.

Phaedra sent him an uncertain, questioning glance.

With Jordana and his comrades staring at him now, too, he scowled and exhaled a low curse. "If we're going, let's get on with it."

He strode past the group, hearing them all fall in behind him, Phaedra included.

Although he didn't like the idea, he had no right to dictate what she did or didn't do. And while it put a boil in his blood, if she decided to take Elijah up on his offer—or any other one the handsome Breed male might have in mind—there was nothing Micah could say about it.

He had no claim on Phaedra at all, even if the persistent thrumming in his veins wanted to balk at that fact.

CHAPTER 11

Slake was packed and pulsing with activity. No surprise, given that the elite club was the pinnacle of Breed gathering places in the city.

Expensive, exclusive, and exceedingly luxe.

Stepping off the elevator from the underground VIP parking garage, Micah and his companions turned a lot of heads despite the crowds already filling the main floor. Being a member of the Order, and dressed in black patrol gear like the other warriors accompanying him, Micah was used to drawing attention.

Inside the elegant club, human blood Hosts—male and female alike—and civilian Breed males from area Darkhavens paused in mid-conversation to watch the group of five warriors and the pair of stunning women in their company cleave a path through the crowd on their way up to the second-floor suite that belonged to Darion.

Micah hardly noticed the stares, except for the ones that followed Phaedra. She was damn hard to miss. As beautiful as Jordana was, with her graceful bearing and long hair the color of moonglow, it was Phaedra's sultry, understated beauty that attracted even more attention. Far more than Micah liked.

He told himself it was only the protector in him— not the stab of sharp possessiveness he felt—that made him place his hand at the small of her back while they ascended the black marble stairs leading up to the higher level of the club. Although she was a powerful, immortal being as well as a gorgeous woman, that didn't mean he wasn't honor-bound to keep her safe.

Especially when he was walking her through a pack of vampires who'd all come to Slake in search of a juicy carotid to tap, along with whatever other cravings they wanted to fill.

No one would dare make a move on her or Jordana, but that didn't mean he shouldn't broadcast the warning anyway.

Yeah, he had a dozen rationalizations for letting his touch linger on her now, but the truth was his blood hadn't stopped burning for her since their interrupted moment outside the archive room.

It was all he could do to keep the embers in his irises from sparking into fire when she looked at him as they reached the second floor of the club. His fangs throbbed in his gums, the sharp points grazing his tongue as he fought to keep all of his unwelcome impulses in check.

Darion entered the unlock code for the suite and invited them all inside. Although neither Micah nor any of his Breed brethren needed artificial light to see, lamps and chandeliers flicked on as the group entered, illuminating the private four-thousand square-foot suite. Open-concept except for the four big bedrooms at the far end, the place had two separate lounge areas with cushioned sectionals and roomy club chairs, a fireplace, billiard table, theater room, and more.

Jordana led Phaedra farther inside. "What do you think?"

"It's bigger than my entire house back home."

The two women walked over to one of the living areas, already chatting like the best of friends as they settled onto the sofa together.

"Who's up to get their ass kicked at the pool table?" Eli asked with a grin.

Micah smirked at his cocky friend. "Sounds like you are."

Jax arched a dark brow. "Teams?"

Eli nodded. "You and me against the three of them seems fair."

Darion chuckled. "Bring it, if you think you can."

"You four go ahead," Nathan said, a glimmer of amusement in the former assassin's eyes. "I'll take on the winning team."

They walked over and set up the first game. As the balls cracked and a familiar banter filled the room, Micah felt himself relaxing for the first time in what felt like forever. He'd trained hard from the minute he was old enough to join the Order. Longer than that, in fact. For nearly as long as he could remember, he'd had a weapon in his hand and a mind set with determination to be the best damned warrior his father had ever seen.

For a while, he thought he'd actually gotten close to achieving that.

Then it all blew up in the Deadlands, along with the men who'd put their trust in him.

His self-directed anger still boiled inside him. When it was his turn at the table again, he sank the striped ball into the pocket with nearly enough force to crack it into pieces.

"Take it easy, brother," Eli chuckled from his post on the receiving end of the table. "This is supposed to be a friendly game, not a death match."

Jax smiled from his place at Eli's side. "Friendly's not exactly his strong suit."

Micah slanted his comrades a wry look, then drove another stripe home. "You ladies gonna yammer the whole time we play? If you're trying to distract me, it won't work."

"Nah," Jax said. "There's only one person here who seems able to distract you, and it's not either of us."

Micah sank a third ball and lifted his narrowed gaze. "What the fuck is that supposed to mean?"

Eli nodded in Phaedra's direction on the other side of the large suite. "You two looked pretty cozy back at headquarters tonight. Something we ought to know?"

"No." Micah scowled, then went back to running the table. Except the next shot he took banked too hard and the ball missed the pocket.

Eli chuckled. "Nope. Clearly, she's not a distraction at all."

Jax moved in to take his turn, grinning along with his teammate. Even Darion looked amused when Micah backed away from the table to join him and Nathan while Jax quickly sank a pair of solid balls in one shot.

"Something funny?"

"No," he said, a smile still tugging at his mouth. "I've just never seen anyone rattle you before, least of all a female."

"I'm not fucking rattled," he snarled under his breath, swiveling his annoyed glower from Darion and Nathan's smug faces to Elijah and Jax. "There's nothing going on between Phaedra and me."

Nor would he allow there to be anything going on, and not only because she would be gone from his life tomorrow.

Eli nodded, looking anything but convinced. "All right, man, whatever you say. I guess you won't mind if Jax or I step in, then."

"Like hell you will." The idea alone made Micah's eyes blaze with amber fire. As much as he liked and respected all of his fellow warriors and friends, none of them were going near Phaedra if he had anything to say about it. "She's way out of your league. She's out of all our leagues."

As he muttered the words, he couldn't help thinking about how incredible it was to see her with the crystal, limned in a silver glow, a look of longing, comfort, and profound love on her beautiful face.

Phaedra was unique from anyone he'd ever known. She was something extraordinary, evidenced not only earlier tonight in the archive room, but also in the kind, selfless work she had devoted herself to back in Rome.

"Micah makes a good point," Darion said, humor gleaming in his eyes. "That on its own should be plenty of reason for you knuckleheads to stand down when it comes to Phaedra, but if it's not, you'll also have destiny to answer to."

"What are you talking about?" Eli asked.

Micah's low growl of warning didn't deter his friend from explaining the highlights from the debriefing they'd sat through together with the Order elders and Zael earlier tonight. Darion summarized the whole thing, from the recurring dream of the white doe to the fact that Micah and Phaedra were apparently cosmically, inextricably connected.

"Soul bonded," Jax said, staring at him as if he just grew a pair of horns.

"It's ridiculous," Micah muttered, glancing toward Phaedra and finding her engrossed in conversation with Jordana.

Eli folded his arms over his chest. "So, you don't believe it's true?"

Fuck, did he? A preordained bond might be the only thing that could help explain the intense, almost magnetic pull Phaedra had on him. How else could he reconcile his visceral attraction to her, even when he'd been convinced she was the enemy?

Deep down, he had to admit the feelings that were taking root in him, while uninvited, were getting stronger, harder to resist, the longer he was near Phaedra.

If their connection was real—if it was some kind of bond destined to bring them together—what would it mean when she returned home tomorrow?

It would mean he'd dodged one hell of a bullet. Phaedra leaving for Rome was the best thing that could happen to him. Soul bond or not, he needed to put a lot of distance between her and all of the troubling cravings he had where she was concerned.

The desire that had almost won out over his discipline in the corridor with her tonight only drove home that point with razor-sharp clarity.

The sooner she could be gone, the better.

He shook his head and bit off a curse. "Are we going to finish this game or what?"

Wisely, his friends gave up busting his balls and took their banter back to the billiard table. Once Micah had control of the shots again, the game was over in a couple of minutes.

Eli came over and clapped Micah on the shoulder. "You know I'd never go after a woman you cared about, right?"

Yeah, he knew that. None of these males would ever cross the line on their brethren.

And while the denial that he cared about Phaedra stayed glued to the roof of Micah's mouth, he gave his fellow warrior a friendly flash of his fangs. "Keep on dreaming that I'd even give you a second's chance to try."

Eli laughed. "Arrogant prick."

"Asshole," Micah said, chuckling along with him.

Jax walked over to them. "I'm heading downstairs to look for a bite. You guys coming?"

Eli nodded. "Hell yes, I'm in."

"Me too," Darion said, then looked at Micah for a response.

Hunger gnawed at him. He'd come to Slake hoping to take the edge off his body's need for more healing red cells, but the thought of going downstairs to select a blood Host from the club's roster of willing and multi-skilled service workers had grown less appealing since they'd arrived in the suite.

He didn't have to wonder if his change of heart—or change of appetite, as it were—had something to do with the temptation of the gorgeous brunette Atlantean who'd been doing her damnedest to ignore him for the past hour.

"I'm good," he murmured. "Maybe I'll catch up with you later."

As the three unmated males left the suite, he felt Nathan's cool stare on him.

"You gonna get on my dick about Phaedra now, too?"

"Not at all." The former Hunter practically vibrated with seriousness. He looked across the long suite to the living area where the two women had been talking nonstop, the bonds of a deep friendship already formed between them. "She's exquisite, isn't she?"

Micah could hardly deny it. "She's beyond that. I've never seen a more beautiful woman in my life. But Phaedra's not just gorgeous. She's good, Nathan. She's just so gentle, so kind. I didn't want to believe it after what happened in the Deadlands, but it seems like I'm the only one trying to prove otherwise. Anyway, fuck me. It doesn't matter. She's going back to Rome tomorrow with Zael and Brynne. That's for the best."

He waited for the cool warrior to agree or to offer some other sage advice, but Nathan stayed silent, unreadable. Then the ghost of a smile edged his mouth.

"Did I say something funny?"

"No, you didn't." Nathan slowly shook his head, his smile growing broader now. "But I was actually talking about Jordana."

"Shit." Micah raked a hand over his head. "You bastard."

Nathan's answering chortle abruptly cut off when the comm unit clipped to his black vest buzzed with an incoming message.

Micah's went off at the same time.

Not even two seconds later, Darion, Eli, and Jax burst back into the suite, their expressions grim with alarm.

"Holy hell," Micah said when his gaze fell to the notification on his device from Gideon at headquarters. "Five Darkhavens in the city are under attack by Rogues."

"It's already chaos downstairs," Eli said, his words punctuated by the sounds of panic and screaming from Slake's other patrons and employees at street level. "Everyone's rushing for the doors."

Nathan read out the Darkhaven addresses Gideon provided in his alert.

"They're all close," Darion said. "Just a few blocks from here."

"I'll get the Rover," Jax said, already starting to pivot away.

"No time," Nathan said.

Micah nodded in agreement. "We'll get there faster on foot."

Jordana and Phaedra both rushed over, less frightened than grave with understanding. Attacks on civilian Breed residences was uncommon, but it happened from time to time. Particularly in recent months, now that the terror group Opus Nostrum had begun weaponizing a narcotic called Red Dragon. The drug accelerated a Breed vampire's blood hunger, sending the Bloodlust-affected victim into a fevered, murderous rage. Too often, the only cure was a brain full of bullets or the business end of a Rogue-killing titanium blade.

"What can we do?" Jordana asked.

"Stay put," Nathan ordered. "You'll be safest up here until we come back, especially with the stampede taking place downstairs."

"Lock the door behind us," Micah added, his gaze locked with Phaedra's. "There's a panic room in the library. If you need it, use it."

Neither Atlantean female looked like they were ready to run and cower, not in the suite and certainly not in a concrete-and-steel-reinforced chamber in a tucked-away corner. If anything, both Phaedra and Jordana looked ready to fight.

"Nathan," Jordana said, but he cut her off with a quick, silencing kiss.

He pressed his comm unit into her hand. "I'll be back for you."

Micah could hardly tear his gaze away from Phaedra's in the moment before he and his brethren took off from the suite, the door banging closed and locked in their wake. Her wide-eyed golden stare was burned into his mind as he, Nathan, Darion, Elijah, and Jax flashed down the stairs then tried to slice through the logjam of a hundred or more Breed civilians and human blood Hosts trying to push their way out the main doors.

The crowd was going nowhere fast, too many bodies attempting to shove through at the same time.

"Side alley," Eli shouted, already racing for the delivery entrance that dumped out to the service street.

"We'll split up once we're outside," Nathan said. "One man to each location."

Micah nodded, mentally triangulating the addresses they'd been given. The Order would no doubt be en route to the attack sites at the same time, but the sooner they had a warrior at each Darkhaven to deal with the Rogues, the fewer civilian casualties they'd be risking.

As they headed for the exit, he tasked everyone with a location. "Eli, you've got Book Hill. Jax, Wisconsin Avenue. Darion, M Street. Nathan, you take Thirtieth. I've got O Street."

The team burst through the service door into the access alley—and immediately found themselves on the end of incoming gunfire.

Snipers on the rooftops.

What the fuck? Based on the hail of bullets flying at them, there had to be close to ten or more assailants. All of them firing down on the warriors like shooting fish in a barrel.

But it was damn hard to hit one of the Breed when they could flash from one spot to another faster than almost any eyes could track. And these idiots had piss-poor aim on top of that.

Micah and the rest of his comrades returned fire as they dodged the bullets raining down on them. He took out a gunman on the building opposite Slake, hitting the son of a bitch in the head. The body tumbled down to the alley in a bloody, broken heap. The scent of Homo sapiens red cells hit Micah's nostrils and he snarled a curse.

"They're humans," he shouted to the others, astonished by the boldness—to say nothing of their apparent death wish. Because these bastards were going down.

Nathan took out two more, one man slumping over the edge of another building, the other body falling to the street.

Evading still more unskilled shots, Micah dropped another assailant while Jax threw a hira-shuriken with one hand and opened fire on a second man with the 9mm in his other. The razor-sharp star sliced a wide gash in the human's throat. As the shooter reached up to stanch the blood flow, he stumbled and plunged from his perch.

Eli shot two more assailants as he danced out of the way of the bullets coming at him from multiple directions.

At that same moment, the side door burst open and some of the patrons from inside the club poured out into the alley.

"Get back!" Micah shouted.

Too late. The group of Breed and human civilians ran straight into the melee. Gunfire from above kept ringing out. One of the fleeing Breed males took a hit. It wasn't severe, but he dropped to the pavement, clutching his arm and howling in agony.

All too soon, Micah realized why.

Light spidered under his skin, creeping up his neck and into his face. The glow of it intensified in mere seconds, spreading like a disease. The Breed male convulsed, light pouring out of his eye sockets as the infiltration rapidly overtook him.

Holy shit.

"UV!" Micah called out. "They've got UV."

Darion wheeled on the growing crowd still flooding into the alley. "Get back inside!"

Chaos erupted as Breed civilians fled, some scattering to the streets, others frantically pushing their way back upstream of the crowd as they ran for the shelter of the club interior. Terrified humans were shoved along with them or trampled underfoot in the sudden chaos.

Micah and his comrades continued unloading on the attackers, one human sniper after another careening lifelessly from their posts. Beside him, Eli bellowed a war cry and let his bullets fly, a pistol in each hand as he dropped two more shooters, then a third.

They ducked behind a dumpster to reload, while in his nearby position in the alley, Darion provided cover. In his peripheral, Micah saw Eli grab for another magazine on his weapon belt. His fingers slowed, then paused. A strange look came into his eyes. He swiveled his head toward Micah, his irises lit with bright sparks from the combat.

Except it wasn't amber light in them.

It was another kind of light.

Micah's blood ran cold. "Ah, Christ. Eli . . ."

Elijah's mouth twisted into an incredulous smirk. "Fuck. I think I'm hit."

The UV began to spread like gasoline through his veins and arteries. He made a strangled noise in the back of his throat, pain contorting his face. It was too late to do anything for him. Too late to stop what was coming as the light sped through his system.

"No," Micah growled. "Goddamn it. No!"

He turned his head away as the warrior's skin and hair ignited. He'd seen a lot of hellish things in his line of work, but he couldn't bear to watch the moment the poisonous UV incinerated his friend.

Micah roared with fury.

Before he could say another word, he was blinded by a sudden burst of shimmering silver light that filled the entire alley.

CHAPTER 12

☾

Cold, bone-deep fear.

That's what Phaedra felt as she and Jordana burst out the side door of the club into the middle of a vicious assault on Micah and the other warriors. Neither she nor Jordana had been comfortable with the order to simply wait behind in a secured suite while the men went off to battle, but then the panic downstairs erupted into full-scale terror when a patron shrieked that the alley was under attack by gunmen with UV rounds.

There hadn't been any reason to doubt it.

Jordana's blood bond to Nathan confirmed the horror taking place outside.

Now, the two women stood side-by-side just outside the door as the civilians scattered out of the alley under a dome of silver Atlantean light that Phaedra had cast over the area with a sweep of her hand.

She didn't know how it happened, or how long she could hold it. All she knew was the still-thrumming presence of the crystal's power—energy that had enveloped her, infused her, from the moment she'd drawn near the crystal earlier tonight—and a desperation to shield Micah and the rest of the Breed warriors and civilians from the incoming barrage of bullets.

Bullets that were somehow enhanced by lethal ultraviolet light.

They kept flying down from several snipers stationed on the surrounding rooftops. But one by one, the rounds hit the exterior of the shield she'd created and disintegrated with harmless puffs of blue smoke.

"Holy shit," Micah said, throwing an astonished glance at her. His eyes glowed hot amber, his Breed pupils transformed to catlike slits and his fangs enormous behind his parted lips.

He looked fierce and savage, menace rolling off him. Yet the expression on his face when he saw her—when he realized what she'd done for him and his friends—was filled with a relief so profound it nearly broke her heart on the spot.

She managed a faint nod, all her focus centered on holding the shimmering light in place.

Jax threw one of his razor-sharp stars at the corner of it, grinning when it ripped through the shield without breaking the barrier. "We can shoot through this. Let's take the rest of these bastards down."

The team opened fire with a vengeance now, safe inside the shelter of her light. Beside Phaedra, Jordana smiled and gave her a grateful nod.

Her palms glowed with otherworldly fire. She unleashed all of it on a gunman who had the poor judgment to unload a volley of now-harmless UV rounds on Nathan's position. The pulse of Atlantean power streaked through the darkness with unfailing aim. The man flew backward off his feet as if he'd been struck by a tsunami, his dying screams echoing over the remaining shooters' assaults.

A shot from Micah's gun took down the last sniper. The body slumped over the edge of the building, his weapon clattering down to the street below.

Silence fell over the alley. The stench of spent rounds, spilled blood, and bitter smoke assaulted Phaedra's nostrils. The carnage had ended. It was over. Thankfully, the awful ambush and the men who'd perpetrated it were no more.

Jordana ran to Nathan, wrapping her arms around him. He held her close, no one uttering a single word.

Despite the quiet, Phaedra couldn't seem to release her hold on the shield of light that protected her new friends . . . and Micah.

He looked at her, his handsome face an unreadable mask in the stillness of the battlefield spread out in all directions on the other side of the sheltering dome. Cast in the silver glow that surrounded him, his gaze was as bleak as she had ever seen it.

"Where's Elijah?" Jordana asked softly, lifting her head from Nathan's chest.

Phaedra had wondered the same thing—until she saw Micah take a step toward a scattered pile of ashes that lay near an old dumpster not far from where the rest of the warriors stood.

Jordana sucked in a sharp breath. "Oh, no. No . . . not Eli."

She started to weep. Phaedra could hardly hold back her emotion, either. Charming, larger-than-life Eli. Gone.

Jax scrubbed a hand over his face, his dark eyes glistening. Darion's sober expression looked controlled on the outside, but his gaze simmered with embers, the tips of his fangs glinting as he bit off a low curse. Even Nathan's measured stare held an edge of shock and grief.

Micah knelt beside the remains of his fallen comrade and retrieved the thick leather belt that bristled with sheathed weapons. Ashes carried on the thin night breeze, skittering across the cracked pavement.

Nathan broke the heavy silence. "I'll call it in to HQ."

As the warrior's deep voice rumbled into his comm unit, Micah rose. Holding Eli's weapon belt in his hand, he walked over to one of the dead gunmen. He kicked the body onto its back, then crouched to remove the rifle and unused ammunition from the dead man.

"UV rounds aren't easy to come by," he commented, as tonelessly as if he were describing the weather.

Nathan's hissed curse drew everyone's attention. He'd ended his call, his normally cool gaze lit with chilling fury. "The reports of the Darkhaven attacks were a ruse. I just got word from Gideon. Lucan, Tegan, Chase, and Brock . . . they rolled out to all four locations and found nothing."

Jax's fangs flashed. "This was a fucking trap. Someone knew we were here and wanted to make sure we had reason enough to come out for the attack."

Darion nodded. "The front exits were jammed for a reason. We were supposed to leave out the side alley, right into their crosshairs."

Phaedra shuddered inside, horrified to imagine the evil it took to concoct such a cruel plan. She couldn't keep her attention from straying to what was left of Eli. In another few moments, the cold breeze would erase him from existence completely.

God, if it had been Micah who'd been taken by one of those UV bullets too . . .

She looked to him, wishing she could run to him the way Jordana had gone to Nathan. Not that Micah needed comforting. She did. She wanted to feel his strong arms around her and feel the reassuring beat of his heart against her cheek.

None of those comforts were hers to want.

Wishing for them now was only selfish, no matter how much she ached with sorrow over the loss of Eli and the fear that it very easily could have been Micah or any one of his brethren—if not all of them.

Micah's vacant gaze slid away from the dead gunman. "This has Opus written all over it."

Nathan gave a grim nod, holding Jordana close. "We need to get back to base."

"I'll get the Rover," Darion said.

Phaedra kept her hold on the light until Nathan stepped over to her with Jordana and laid his hand gently on her shoulder. "Thank you," he said soberly. "It's time to get you and Jordana out of here now."

She glanced past him to where Micah and Jax were carefully collecting the fallen snipers' weapons and ammunition. On Nathan's nod, she lowered her hand and the alley plunged into darkness.

CHAPTER 13

There was no talk of Eli's death when they returned. The anguishing news had already reached the Order's headquarters from Nathan's call in the alley. The women's faces were drawn with shock and grief, but Lucan and the rest of the warriors greeted the returning team with a solemn, yet determined, urgency.

"Let's get to work," he announced gravely. "Daybreak will be here soon. We've got roughly twelve hours to prepare for nightfall and the pain we're going to send back to Opus for what they did tonight."

Phaedra had never felt so helpless or bereft as she did watching Micah and his comrades file soberly into their war room together with the Order elders and Zael, then quietly close the door behind them.

Micah hadn't uttered a word the entire drive back to the mansion. Phaedra knew Eli's death was a void that couldn't be filled, not with conversation or sorrow. But the stoic response he'd shown in the alley had hardened into a stony withdrawal by the time they arrived at headquarters.

He'd retreated to a dark place, and the look in his eyes chilled her to her marrow.

It was the same bleakness she'd seen in his gaze when he spoke to her about his psychic ability to hear the worst of mankind's thoughts and sins. The same bleakness that seemed to live somewhere inside him, and made her worry that if he sank any deeper into that abyss, eventually, he might not come back.

Was the fear she felt for him just part of the soul bond that neither of them wanted to acknowledge? Did that explain how she could be coming to care for him so deeply after only a couple days' time?

In truth, he'd been seared into her consciousness— into her heart—from the moment they came face-to-face in the Deadlands more than a week ago. She had worried for him, mourned him when she believed he'd been killed along with his men.

She hadn't wanted to feel anything for the angry, violent man she'd encountered in the Rome command center, but destiny, and her heart, had given her little choice.

Concern for Micah stayed with her for the next couple of hours. Although Jordana, Jenna, Gabrielle, and the rest of the women had tried to make her feel welcome by inviting her to sit and talk with them in the tranquil setting of the residence's library, she had been too restless to stay for long.

Instead, she wandered the corridors of the massive command center, torn between wishing she had never left her quiet life in Rome and dreading the dwindling hours before she would have to leave to return.

One thing she knew for certain was she couldn't go without seeing Micah, whether he wanted her company or not.

The warriors' meeting had broken up several minutes ago. She'd heard the rumble of deep voices in one of the labyrinthine corridors as she paced an aimless path up one hallway to the next. She didn't know where to look for Micah in the maze of the compound, or even if she were permitted to be there.

Rounding a corner, she nearly collided with the big, muscled frame of Darion Thorne.

"Oh. I'm sorry, I was just—"

He frowned as she gaped up at him. His gaze was too knowing, and filled with warning. "He's not in a good place right now. You probably don't want to be near him."

She let go of the breath she was holding. "No, probably not. Do you know where he is?"

Darion's mouth softened, though not by much. He gestured to the empty corridor behind him. "I saw him in the weapons room a few minutes ago. Halfway down, can't miss it. And Phaedra," he added, as she started to walk past him. "Thank you for what you did tonight. If Micah won't say the words, just know that all of us—the entire Order—is in your debt."

She gave him a sad smile, wishing she'd been able to help Eli too. "Thank you, Darion."

He nodded, his innate honor and confident bearing so much like his formidable father's.

"Just be careful," he said, then continued up the corridor.

Phaedra headed in the direction he'd indicated, her feet slowing as she reached an open doorway of a room stocked with enough weapons and ammunition to outfit the army of a small country. Guns, blades, chains . . . even a wall lined with a dozen swords of various lengths.

As she stepped inside, she saw there was an adjacent room set up for target practice. Cold fluorescent lights bathed the long, windowless rectangular space in a harsh, clinical glow.

And there, standing opposite of the targets at the back of the range, was Micah.

On one of the tables behind him were the large pistols he'd used earlier tonight, now cleaned and disassembled. On another table lay an array of terrible-looking blades. He was still dressed in his black combat gear, the scent of smoke and ash hanging thinly in the air.

Without acknowledging she was there, he picked up one of the daggers and threw it at the target dummy at the far end of the range. It struck dead-on in the center of the dummy's chest, sinking all the way to the hilt.

"You shouldn't be in here."

Phaedra took a step past the threshold. "I wanted to make sure you were all right."

He still wouldn't look at her, but she saw a tendon jump in the side of his cheek in response to her quiet expression of concern. "I'm just fucking peachy. Another of my friends got ashed, Opus Nostrum set us up, left us standing around with our dicks in our hands, and there's not a goddamned thing I can do about it until the sun goes down tomorrow."

He picked up another blade and sent it flying. The hard thump as it hit home between the dummy's eyes made Phaedra flinch. He retrieved a third dagger and sent it after that one, then another, and another. The target dummy exploded from the rapid-fire impacts, chunks of flesh-like rubber flying in all directions at the other end of the range.

Micah's breath sawed out of him. His deep voice took on a sharper, more dangerous edge. "I'll say it one more time. You should not be in here with me."

"I know that." She walked forward, her steps cautious but unyielding. "I know you prefer to be alone, Micah. I know you think you don't need anyone, that you have to bear all of this pain alone. But you don't."

He blew out a caustic laugh and turned to reach for another weapon to launch but there were none left. His back to her, he snarled, "If you're expecting me to swallow more of your Atlantean soul bond fairy tales, save your breath. I live in the real world."

"So do I, Micah. I live in the same world you do. The one where there's pain and ugliness and death. The same world, where there's loss so sharp and deep that when it comes, it hollows out a part of you that you can never get back."

He stilled as Phaedra stepped closer to him. "Losing your parents to an accident centuries ago isn't the same as losing five of your closest friends because of your own negligence. It's not the same as watching Eli fry right before my fucking eyes tonight."

"No, it isn't," she admitted. "But I wasn't talking about my parents. I was talking about my husband."

When he swung toward her, she realized why he had avoided looking at her until now. His eyes were lit with fiery sparks. His pupils had thinned to the narrowest vertical slits in the middle of all that amber fire.

"Your husband." The growled words might have been a question, but the sharpness in his expression made it seem almost an accusation. "What about fate and destiny?"

She shook her head. "Niccolo was mortal. We met after I left the colony to live in Rome. My husband was a kind, good man. Only a few years after we fell in love, I learned he was killed in the street after he tried to stop another man from beating his wife. If I had been with Niccolo—if I had been able to use my hands to stop his killing . . ." She looked down at her palms, at the faint glow that rose in them when she thought about Niccolo's murder. "But I wasn't there. After I lost him, I felt so powerless. I felt so terribly alone. Eventually, I realized I could do something after all. There were ways I could help other people, like the women and children who have nowhere else to go. I could do something to save them."

Micah remained silent, his unblinking gaze searing. Then he smiled, baring those deadly fangs as if to remind her of the predator that lived inside him. "Is that what this is about? Is that why you came down here to find me? You think you can rescue me, Phaedra?"

She flinched at his cutting tone. The words stung, but so did the way he seemed so intent on pushing her away. He moved from where he stood near the table, his big body vibrating with dark challenge.

Prowling closer, he curled his lips back from his fangs on a dangerous smile. "You think I need saving?"

She knew he did. Deep down in the most tender corner of her soul, she knew she might be all that stood between Micah and the only thing powerful enough to destroy him.

Himself.

She just wasn't sure her heart was strong enough to try.

"I don't know why I told you any of this. It doesn't matter, not to you, anyway. No one matters to you, not even yourself. You'd rather wallow in your grief and anger alone." She shook her head, sad for him and furious at herself for being foolish enough to care when he didn't. "You're right, Micah. I shouldn't be in here with you."

When she turned to leave, his hand clamped around her wrist. Her breath halted at the contact. Her heart started to gallop, pounding so hard it was practically all she could hear. Micah's strong fingers were like warm bands of iron that she wouldn't have been able to break out of if she tried.

But she didn't try.

No matter how furious the urge was to save herself—and her heart—from breaking with this dangerous male, she didn't put up any fight when he turned her around to face him.

In his eyes, an inferno raged.

His fangs were enormous, the razor tips gleaming bright white as he pulled in a rasping breath, then hissed it out on a curse.

"Is this your fate, Phaedra? Is this what your precious destiny wants for you?"

Looking at him like this, with burning fury in his eyes and dark, lethal power in both his grip on her and in the dominating heat of his immense body, she couldn't think of any cosmic reason for the two of them to have been thrust together.

And yet, he was the only man who had ever stirred such a wild longing in her. The only man she had felt was somehow a part of her from the moment their eyes clashed for the first time in the Dreamscape.

Fear and confusion made her palms warm with the rising of her power. Not the shielding light she had cast over the alley tonight, but the pulsing glow that she and every other Atlantean could wield as a weapon.

Micah must have felt the vibration through his hold on her. He knew what she could do. He'd watched Jordana throw her punishing light at the snipers who'd been firing on them outside Slake.

But Micah showed no fear with Phaedra. No, he seemed to welcome her ire.

Drawing her closer with his grasp still locked on her wrist, he brought her clenched, glowing fist up near his face. "Do it, Phaedra. God knows, I've given you enough reason."

She made a small noise in her throat, one part protest, one part foolish, desperate hope.

Hope that he would let her go.

Hope that he wouldn't.

His gaze seared her. A low growl built in his chest when she refused to give him what he demanded. He ground out her name like a curse. Then he hauled her against him and his mouth closed over hers in a hot, unforgiving kiss.

The shock of his lips on hers sent liquid fire rushing through her. The crush of his muscled body against her curves ignited every nerve ending, spreading like an electric current into her breasts, her limbs, her core. He was hard against her, his arousal an unmistakable ridge against her hip. She moaned and it was a hungry, shameless sound, one she couldn't have held back if her life depended on it.

Micah tore his mouth away from hers on a snarl. "You shouldn't have saved me, Phaedra. Not in that alley tonight. Not back in those Deadlands." He scowled, his blazing eyes scorching her with rage and desire. "You're the reason I survived that blast. I think I knew it then. After tonight, I'm fucking certain of it."

Had she saved him from the detonation that killed his team?

Was that why fate had put her in the Deadlands with him—because the power of the crystals would never harm her, and his proximity to her had somehow shielded him from the worst of the blast as well?

He wanted to believe their destiny was a mistake. She had struggled to accept it could be true, too, but not anymore. Not when the thought of him dying ripped open an ache inside her that she felt all the way to her soul.

"I was so scared tonight, Micah." The whispered admission gusted out of her. "After it was over, all I wanted to do was run to you and never let go."

She knew he had little use for tenderness or soft emotions, but she couldn't hold the words back. His expression hardened as he studied her, but his hand on her wrist and the one now cupping her nape remained.

"And now?" he rasped. "What is it you want now, Phaedra?"

"This. You." She swallowed, already gone too far and unwilling to retreat. "I want you."

His wordless reply rumbled against her like thunder. It was all the warning he gave her before he lowered his head and took her mouth once more.

There was fire in this kiss too.

There was demand.

His tongue invaded her parted lips, the fevered strokes stirring a wild need inside her. She knew where this kiss was heading. It had been a lifetime since she'd been with a man, but never had her desire erupted so swiftly into raw, urgent need.

On a moan, she melted against him, pulling her hand free of his loose hold so she could bring her arms up around his broad shoulders and hold him closer while he claimed her mouth in a blistering, soul-shattering kiss.

The hand that released hers skimmed beneath the hem of her shirt. The first brush of his fingertips against the bare skin of her belly made her shudder with desire. When he moved higher, palming the sensitive mound of her breast, all of the heated need coiling inside her spiraled into her core.

Micah broke their kiss, but only for a moment, drawing back to look at her. The molten glow of his transformed irises felt as hot as a caress on her face.

"I told you that you shouldn't have come in here with me," he murmured. "If you have second thoughts, you'd better voice them now."

Her breath was racing, shallow pants that matched the speeding rate of her pulse. She couldn't find her voice, but she had no need for words. Spearing her fingers into his short hair, she pulled his head down to meet hers and let her hungered kiss tell him everything he needed to know.

"Ah, fuck," he snarled into her mouth.

His hips bucked forward, driving the rigid length of his erection against her. His free hand went between her legs, caressing her sex over her clothing. She wanted to feel his touch on her skin. Faith, she wanted that and more.

As if he knew what she craved, Micah deftly unbuttoned her dark jeans and tugged the zipper down. His fingers dipped into her cleft, and he let out a jagged breath when he found her wetness.

"Christ, you're soft. So silky and hot."

She whimpered a response, but it was lost as soon as he began to stroke her tender flesh. When he teased the tight bud of her clit, she cried out, aching for the release his touch promised.

Micah kissed her deeper now, using those skillful fingers to bring her to the brink of shattering. Beside her, she heard the door of the windowless target range close and lock on his mental command. Then cool air hit her backside as her jeans and panties fell to the floor beneath her. A moment later, her feet lifted off the floor and all her weight was held aloft on Micah's powerful hands.

She didn't know how he'd managed to free himself from his own pants, but the thick shaft of his cock now replaced his fingers as he stroked against the slick folds of her sex. Pressing her back to the wall, he rolled his pelvis into hers in a hard grind, his eyes smoldering.

"I need to be inside you," he rasped thickly, his fangs filling his mouth.

Phaedra could only pant her reply. "Yes. Now."

His jaw clenched in response. Shifting against her, he angled himself into position. Then, with his eyes locked on hers, he slowly filled her, inch by heart-stopping inch.

She couldn't help the carnal sound that exploded from her lips.

He felt too big for her, too wild. And he showed her no mercy at all.

Raw pleasure shot through her body at the ferocity of him. Her head fell back as he moved inside her, his hard, urgent thrusts breaking something open inside her, flooding her senses with an ecstasy she had never known. All of that sensation swelled to overflowing, too intense to contain.

Micah gave her no quarter. His tempo was aggressive and unapologetic, driving her to the edge of oblivion with every relentless stroke.

She welcomed every crushing pound of his body into hers. She needed it every bit as much as he seemed to. More.

Primal, unleashed power radiated from him, all of that dangerous strength and fury as shocking as a storm. It made her ache to be consumed. To be obliterated by the savageness of his passion for her.

Her senses careened like a leaf caught in a tempest, sensation like lightning in her veins and in every fiber of her being. She had no choice but to let the pleasure pour over her.

She cried out as the need inside her exploded into a release that rocked her to her soul.

CHAPTER 14

☾

He knew it had been a mistake to let Phaedra anywhere near him tonight, but damn if he could conjure even a shred of remorse when he was buried to the hilt in her soft body.

Her orgasm broke over her in violent waves. He'd never seen anything more beautiful than Phaedra's face gripped in release. The fact that he had been the one to give her that pleasure made him feel like a god.

More than a god, for those prolonged moments as she trembled against him, her tiny muscles gripping his cock like a fist, he felt as if she actually had been preordained to belong to him.

Soul bonded.

Fated mates.

All his dismissive comments and denials about destiny having a hand in bringing them together tasted as dry as ashes in the back of his throat when Phaedra opened her dusky golden eyes and held his stare as he thrust inside her.

"This feels so good," she whispered, her lids drifting closed again as an aftershock contracted around his length in tiny ripples. "I wanted it to last, but I've never . . . I didn't know how good it could be."

He grunted, a smile tugging at the corner of his mouth. "Don't worry, I'm nowhere close to finished with you."

He wasn't willing to pull out of her heat either. With his unfastened patrol fatigues sagged around his hips and his arms still holding her astride him, he swung her away from the wall and carried her to the edge of the empty weapons table.

Not the most romantic place he could think of, but his need for her was too impatient to care. All he knew was the pounding desire that flared even brighter as Phaedra reached for his face and brought him down for her kiss.

His chest pressed into her softness, their clothing rasping between them with each hard thrust of his body into hers. He wanted to be naked with her. He wanted to take it slow and savor every breathless moan that spilled off her lips, every delicious tremor that shook her as she moved beneath him.

That's what he wanted, but his desire for her refused its leash.

He took her fast and hard and deep.

She fit him perfectly, and as the wet friction of their joining ratcheted his need closer and closer to the breaking point, his pulse hammered like a war drum, blood surging through his veins. His heart pounded with a rhythm that seemed to roar a single word: Mine.

He'd felt that wild possessiveness even before this moment.

God help her, she'd belonged to him from the instant he spotted her in those scorched, barren woods.

After tonight, a part of her would always belong to him, although something reckless and untamed inside him wanted nothing less than all of her. A cowardly craving, and not only because she was leaving tomorrow for the life she'd left behind in Rome.

He wanted her in spite of the fact that she did not—and could never—be his in any true sense of the word. The Order was his calling. It was his life. He had made his choice from the time he was old enough to hold a weapon in his hand.

Fate and destiny be damned, but beautiful, kind-hearted Phaedra had no place with him.

Except like this, right here and now.

Her pleasured cries as he brought her to another explosive climax made his own release gather and build. He couldn't get close enough, couldn't get deep enough into the yielding softness of her body's tight sheath. Lifting his head on a thick roar, he watched her lovely face as she quivered and sighed his name. His vision burned with the bright amber that devoured his irises. His fangs filled his mouth, the dagger-sharp points digging into his tongue as he clenched his teeth and snarled with the jolting rush of his hot seed as it exploded inside her.

She arched off the table on a strangled scream, her hands clutching the back of his head, her thighs wrapped around his waist. Her body shook, soft sounds of surrender in the shallow sighs that fanned against his ear. Christ, he didn't know how she managed to feel both as fragile as a kitten and as fierce as a goddess in his arms. It was an addicting combination, one that could easily consume him.

That she was immortal, part of a race of beings he'd long considered his enemy, was only a fraction of what made his desire for Phaedra so dangerous to him. It was her tender heart, her innate goodness, that had awakened something disturbing inside him.

She had begun to make him long for something more than the vengeance he'd vowed to have for the deaths of his teammates in the Deadlands. And, now, he had to add Eli's slaying to that grim tally.

That vengeance should have been all that mattered to him.

The grief and guilt he carried for all of those lost lives would never go away, not even after he had the retribution he was prepared to give his life in order to have.

His dedication to that goal hadn't faltered.

But if he wasn't careful, his feelings for Phaedra were going to keep staking more territory. He only had room for duty. For cold, merciless payback.

Or so he told himself, as his climax ebbed, only to flare back to life with even greater ferocity.

It staggered him, how savagely he wanted her all over again.

His need for her was animal, a feral hunger that he'd never known before.

"Mine," he uttered roughly against her mouth, even though he knew it was no better than a lie.

She couldn't be his. In a few hours she would be leaving and he would resume the life he'd been born and raised to lead.

Regardless of all those truths, he said the reckless word again, unable to bite it back. "Mine, Phaedra."

She gasped his name on a broken sigh, and he was lost to that wild, predatory need.

He wanted her. All the way to his marrow, he wanted her.

God help him, now that he'd been inside her, he was going to crave her every day of his eternal life.

As his arousal surged with renewed greed for her, he didn't know whether to curse the dawn that would take her away from him in the morning, or pray to hell it arrived soon.

CHAPTER 15

☪

When Phaedra woke up at daybreak alone in the big bed of her guest room, she thought for a moment that making love with Micah had only been a dream. A fantastic dream, at that.

As soon as she moved on the soft mattress, all the little aches and dull throbs between her legs and elsewhere told her he'd been no dream. And she couldn't really call the raw passion they'd shared making love, either. It had been something bigger. Something explosive and uncontrolled.

A primal, undeniable connection that still vibrated in her marrow.

In her very soul.

She had been so drunk on pleasure she hardly remembered walking back to her room with him after they'd rearranged their clothing and he'd escorted her through the empty corridors of the command center. The hard, still-hungered kiss he'd given her at her door had left the ghost of a bruise on her lips. She ran the tip of her tongue over the tenderness that lingered there now, savoring the reminder of Micah's passion.

It was a bittersweet reminder, because although he hadn't said as much, incredible as their time together was last night, it also felt like a goodbye.

Now that dawn had come, it might only be a scant handful of hours before she would be departing for Rome with Zael and Brynne. She didn't know if Micah would seek her out before then. Her head said he wouldn't, but her heart was filled with a foolish sense of hope.

After telling herself nearly since she'd arrived at the Order's headquarters that she couldn't wait to return home, now she found herself merely going through the motions of preparing to leave.

She took a long shower, then dressed for the imminent trip. Her small bag didn't require much packing, so after arranging her long chestnut hair into a loose ponytail, she left her room to look for Zael and his mate.

She found them seated with Jordana in a cozy garden courtyard just outside the mansion's large kitchen. As soon as Brynne saw Phaedra approaching the French doors that opened onto the sunlit stone patio, she motioned for Phaedra to join them.

"There you are," Zael's daywalker mate said, greeting her with a warm smile. "After the night you had, we were reluctant to wake you too early for breakfast."

Faith, did they all know what she'd been doing with Micah? Phaedra hadn't blushed in nearly a thousand years, but she couldn't help the little jolt of embarrassment that seeped into her face.

She sat down in the vacant chair Brynne had indicated. The table had been set with a basket of freshly baked croissants and pastries, as well as a carafe of delicious-smelling coffee and a pot of aromatic tea.

"Please, help yourself," Brynne said, nudging the basket of baked goods toward her.

Phaedra placed an apple-stuffed pastry on her plate, then poured some tea into the delicate bone china cup in front of her. As she took a sip, she felt all three pairs of eyes studying her in curious silence.

"How are you feeling?" Jordana asked, tilting her head.

"I'm fine. Is anything wrong?"

Even Zael appeared concerned. His golden brows furrowed over his tropical blue eyes. "I've never known anyone who could cast light the way Jordana says you did last night."

"Oh." So that's what this was about. Phaedra exhaled, her awkwardness instantly put aside. "I didn't realize I could do it, either."

Zael grunted. "It's an extraordinary gift. Not even your parents had that kind of power."

"They didn't?"

He slowly shook his head. "You had no idea you had this ability?"

She set her teacup down. "I didn't think I'd been born with any particular gifts, other than the one all Atlanteans possess, to wield the energy that lives in our palms."

"That's gift enough for anyone, but this . . ." He stared at her in quiet contemplation for a moment.

"Have you ever held one of the crystals in your hands before?"

"Never. Selene had forbidden anyone to touch the five that belonged to the realm, as I'm sure you know. The one that was taken to the colony was always kept under protection there, too. I never had any reason to touch any of the crystals."

He nodded. "But your connection to them is unique among all of our people, Phaedra. Even Selene. Your parents gave a piece of themselves to create those power sources that have protected Atlantis and given our people the enduring light we require to survive. Maenos and Sindarah are a part of the crystals. By extension, so are you."

"Do you have any idea how remarkable you are?" Brynne asked.

Jordana nodded, her expression a mix of gratitude and awe. "If you hadn't been there last night, we would have lost everyone. If you hadn't done what you did, Phaedra, I would have lost Nathan."

Yet for all their astonishment and praise, the three of them seemed too sober for her peace of mind. "What aren't you telling me?"

"The light," Zael said. "That kind of power cannot be wielded without consequences. Any time one of us uses the power in our palms, it sends a ripple of energy through the rest of our people. It does not go unnoticed by any of our kind."

Phaedra swallowed. She knew that, of course. It was a common acceptance among all Atlanteans, a truth she rarely considered because it was beyond rare that she ever summoned the light that lived in her hands.

Not because she had any reason to hide, but because she had willingly given up her Atlantean ways when she'd decided to make her life among the mortals with Niccolo all those decades ago.

Over the centuries, she had heard tales about Selene's loyal soldiers using the energy trails of errant Atlantean fugitives in order to track them down and execute traitors to the realm. Phaedra had never feared for her own life when it came to the queen. Selene's respect for Maenos and Sindarah had given Phaedra limited leeway with her, even after Phaedra had fled the realm for the colony.

But Zael and the members of the Order?

Selene would give no quarter to any of them.

"Oh, no. I've exposed you all to her wrath now. She has to know where I am, that I'm here with you and the Order." She pushed her plate away, her appetite suddenly dried up. Her stomach pitched and rolled with the dread of what she'd done. "I never should've come here. Zael, you need to get me out of here right away. It won't be safe for anyone if I stay. Selene will trace me here and send her legion straight to this compound to attack."

He calmly placed his hand over hers. "If Selene wants to instigate a war with the Order, she will already be taking steps to make it happen. I can tell you from experience that she's had that opportunity already, but stayed her hand."

Brynne nodded in agreement, exchanging a private look with Zael before glancing at Phaedra. "What we can't afford to risk now is that she might come after you for information to help her plan such an attack."

"Or find a way to use your power against us," Zael added.

That thought, more than any concern for her own safety, chilled her to her bones. "So, what does this mean, then?"

"You can't go back to Rome now, Phaedra. It won't be safe for you. It especially won't be safe for the Order. Lucan has already made the decision. He feels, and I agree, the best place you can be is here, under the Order's protection. Under my personal protection as well."

She couldn't argue with the logic, but she had responsibilities waiting for her back home. She had people in dangerous situations of their own who relied on her to keep them safe from harm. "What about the shelter? The women and children—"

Brynne nodded. "We've already informed Lazaro of the change in plans. Sia and Trygg will be relocating to your house to manage things until it's safe for you to return."

"When might that be?"

The fact that neither Brynne nor Zael had that answer for her only reinforced the seriousness of what the Order was facing. And now she had added to those troubles.

She could hardly stand the idea that by trying to protect Micah and the other warriors, instead she had potentially endangered them all.

"I don't think I can eat right now," she murmured, rising from the table on shaky legs. "Will you all excuse me, please?"

CHAPTER 16

It had only been a few hours since he'd been inside Phaedra and he already wanted her again.

Or, rather, still.

After seeing her to her guest room, he'd spent the remainder of the time before dawn bagging the remains of the target dummy in the weapons room, then trying to drown his hunger for Phaedra under an ice-cold shower for nearly an hour.

It hadn't worked.

The only hope he had left was the four thousand miles that would be placed between them once she was delivered back to her home in Rome.

He had done his damnedest to steer clear of her, keeping busy down in the command center with Jax and Darion, and avoiding stepping foot in the mansion's residence. The pair of nines he wore on his weapons belt had never been cleaner. The handcrafted titanium blade he'd dropped in a nomad's village after dragging himself across miles of Siberian wilderness—the blade his father had returned to him—had been sharpened to the finest edge it had ever seen.

He glanced up from polishing the blade for the hundredth time and found Darion staring at him, a look of wry amusement on his face.

"Why don't you just go talk to her?"

Micah went back to cleaning a nonexistent smudge from the blade. "Talk to who?"

"The female who's got your dick in a knot."

"She'll be leaving soon for Rome with Zael and Brynne." He looked at his friend and shrugged. "It's for the best."

Darion arched a dark brow. "The fact that you're not even trying to deny there's something going on between you and Phaedra says it all."

He set the dagger down on the table harder than intended. "You got a point to make here, Dare?"

"Holy hell. You care about her."

"Of course, he does," Jax said, pausing his hira-shuriken target practice to weigh in. The fury that had cloaked them all after Eli's killing had galvanized into a cold purpose for the slain warrior's patrol partner. Despite his grief, Jax slid a smirk in Micah's direction. "You can't fight destiny, brother."

Was that all it was?

Could this magnetic pull he felt toward Phaedra be explained away so easily?

Was his desire for her simply a product of the Dreamscape and some predetermined assertion that they were meant to be? Or did his feelings for her run deeper than some illusionary edict neither of them had any control over?

Nothing about last night felt that simple to dismiss.

The way her presence called to him now felt too real to be discounted as just some cosmic matchmaking gone awry.

And that made it all the more critical for him to keep his distance.

Four thousand miles would be a decent start.

It would have to be. And the sooner, the better.

"She's probably packing up to go as we speak," he said, feeling like a first-class asshole for purposely allowing her to leave without a word from him after what they'd shared a few hours ago. "Phaedra doesn't belong here. She doesn't belong with me. As for destiny, it's got no fucking place here, either."

His sharp statement was punctuated by the vibrating buzz of his comm unit. He brought it to his ear and listened as Lucan Thorne summoned him for a one-on-one in the commander's study upstairs.

"Yes, sir." He slipped the device back into his pocket and shot a glance at his friends. "Duty calls."

Not a minute too soon, as far as he was concerned. The last thing he wanted to do was stand around talking about his feelings.

Eli's slaying and the ambush Opus Nostrum had executed demanded a swift and violent answer. If Micah had anything to say about it, he wanted to be on the front lines of the response.

Then he could get back to the business of dealing with whatever had attacked him and his team in the Deadlands a week ago.

With those thoughts putting a hard purpose in his stride, he headed up the corridor.

As he rounded a corner, he spotted Jenna coming out of the archive room. She held her fingers to her temples, then she leaned into the jamb of the open doorway.

Micah rushed to her side. "Are you okay?"

"Yeah, I think so." She frowned, slowly regaining her balance. "I'm okay."

"You were feeling off last night too," he reminded her.

"It's nothing. Just a little woozy, like someone's scratching at the inside of my skull. It comes and goes. I'll feel better if I lie down for a few minutes."

"Come on, I'll walk you to your quarters."

"You don't have to."

"I think I do, Jenna." He held out his arm, fully expecting her to refuse. The fact that she didn't raised more than a little concern in him. He walked her to the elevator, her arm still looped through his as they rode up to the main level. "Does Brock know you've been feeling like this?"

She gave a small laugh. "My overprotective mate knows everything."

As if on cue, Brock was waiting outside the elevator doors as they opened. He reached in and gathered Jenna close.

"Thanks, man," he said, giving Micah a grateful nod as the couple walked out together to make their way to their quarters.

Micah watched them for a moment, trying to ignore the pang of guilt he felt for dodging Phaedra. He'd never thought of himself as a coward, but damn if he wasn't acting like one with her.

She had saved his life—twice, by his count. Last night, she'd saved the lives of three of his friends. And then she'd topped off that miracle by giving him the incredible gift of her body. She had given him the honor of her pleasure, uninhibited, and so fucking honest, he would never be able to lay with another woman without comparing everything to Phaedra.

At the very least, he owed her a few words before she was gone from his life forever.

Her guest room was just down the hallway from Jenna and Brock's quarters.

The door was open, as it had been the last time he'd stood there. At first, he didn't see her. Then she stepped out of the walk-in closet with an empty hanger in her hand, about to make her way over to her travel bag that sat open on the bed.

She froze when she saw him. "Micah."

"Hello, Phaedra." He forced himself to stay outside the room, no matter how strong the urge was to get close to her. He'd already done enough of that, and seeing her soft expression as she stared at him now was only inviting more trouble. He cleared his throat. "I'm on my way to meet with Lucan, so I've only got a minute."

"Okay." A hesitant smile played at the edge of her lips. "Would you like to come in?"

"No."

It was a lie and then some. He tried not to notice the look of stung confusion that crept into her eyes as he stood there, unmoving on the other side of the threshold. It was the right thing to do. Especially when everything male inside him craved nothing more than a further taste of her.

He didn't need any stronger reason to keep his boots planted where they were than the flare of arousal licking through him as he stared at Phaedra.

"I came by because I wanted to apologize for last night."

"Apologize?"

He gave her a rueful smile. "I know you think I'm incapable, but when I'm wrong, I do own up for it. What I did last night with you was wrong. I wanted you, Phaedra. Fuck, I've wanted you from the moment I saw you in that Deadlands forest. But it was wrong to give in to that desire. It was selfish, and I truly am sorry for that."

She set down the hanger she'd been holding and slowly crossed the room to approach him. "I don't want an apology. I'm not sorry for last night."

She stepped closer, until there was barely an arm's length between them. Her sweet fragrance engulfed him, put his senses into a tailspin. Even out of reach, he could feel the warmth of her skin. He could smell sunshine in her upswept hair.

Another step brought her right in front of him, and it was all he could do not to touch the satin softness of her bared neck where her pulse fluttered. His gums prickled with the stirring of his fangs. He ground his molars together, fighting the temptation to taste that ticking vein, along with all of the other impossible urges he had where she was concerned.

Her pretty mouth curved with a small smile. "Don't say you're sorry, Micah. I've never felt so alive as I did last night with you."

He groaned, low in his throat. He had been hoping she'd make this easier on him—tell him she'd made a terrible mistake letting him anywhere near her, scream at him to stay the fuck away from her, or maybe slam the door in his face as soon as she saw him standing there.

He had been prepared for her outrage or contempt. She'd be justified in either one. He'd even been prepared for her tears and recriminations.

But not this.

Steeling himself to her sweetness was more difficult than facing off against an army of enemies. She looked so beautiful as she waited for his reply, so damn vulnerable. She was an ageless, powerful being, yet she stood before him with an uncertainty in her gentle eyes that said he could break her with a careless word.

He blew out a curse, raking his hand over his head. "Being with you was amazing. I'm not going to say it wasn't. But it shouldn't have happened. It was on me to keep my distance, and I fucked that up."

"Micah, that's not what I wanted—"

"I shouldn't have let it happen," he snapped, needing to say the words quickly, before he caved to the urge to draw her into his arms. "I can't tell you I regret a second of what we did, because I don't."

"Then what are you trying to say?"

"Fuck. I don't know." His head jammed up with all the things he couldn't say to her. How extraordinary he thought she was. What a jackass he'd been with her from the start. How sadistic fate must be to throw them together the way they had been, with their lives on two opposite paths—hers, waiting for her back in Rome, and his on a battlefield that was only getting bloodier and deadlier by the hour.

That's why it could only end now, before he waded any deeper into his caring for her. The best thing that could happen to either one of them now was for Phaedra to be as far away from him as possible.

He gave a harsh shake of his head. "I guess I'm just here to say goodbye."

She tilted her head, her brow creasing with her frown. "You haven't heard?"

"Heard what?"

"I'm not leaving. Zael and Brynne just told me a few minutes ago."

"What do mean you're not leaving? Why not?"

The confusion drained from her expression as she stared at him, replaced by something else. Something that looked a lot like pain. "I have to stay here. When I shielded everyone in the alley, I also exposed my location to Selene and all the rest of my people. I'll be a target now, and some might try to use me as a weapon against the Order. Lucan has decided, and Zael agrees, the safest thing for everyone is for me to stay here, under the protection of the Order."

"Holy shit."

He gaped at her, alarm spiking through him as he processed what he was hearing. She hadn't been packing to leave; she had been ordered to stay. Because of him. Phaedra was in danger now because she'd helped him and his friends. That selfless act had put a bullseye on her back. Micah's blood ran cold at the thought of anyone going after her.

Selene. Her legion of loyal guards. Opus.

The list was too long, and too lethal.

Now he understood Lucan's summoning him to his study. Micah wouldn't be surprised if the Order's shrewd leader didn't already have some inkling of the attraction boiling out of control between Phaedra and him. Hell, his father probably had some choice words waiting for him too—not only as a parent, but as one of the Order's top commanders.

"Fuck." Micah let the curse explode out of him. "I have to go."

"You're disappointed." Phaedra took a step back. "No, you're more than disappointed."

He scowled. "I'm pissed at myself. For last night, for letting things get so out of control between us. For the fact that you had to risk yourself to help me and my friends. I'm pissed at myself for the way you're looking at me right now. I never should've let any of it happen."

A quiet breath fell from her lips. "Oh. I see. Now I'm beginning to understand. You only wanted me because you thought I was leaving."

He stood there mutely as she moved farther away from him. He wouldn't lie to her and say that hadn't been part of what allowed him to give in to his need for her. But he would have wanted her regardless of whether she left or stayed.

He wanted her even now.

To keep from reaching out to her, he fisted his hands at his sides. He clamped his jaw tight in order to keep from saying things to reassure her. Things that would only make it harder for him to keep his distance now that she would be living under the same roof with him for God only knew how long.

His comm unit buzzed in his pocket. He didn't have to look to know it was Lucan.

Phaedra continued to stare at him, a firmness settling into her proud chin. That's how he knew she was really hurt. The tender, open-hearted kindness that was so much a part of her began to shutter as the moments passed and the drone of his incoming summons continued to pulse in the silence between them.

She blinked, and he caught a glimpse of the formidable immortal that was also part of the special woman he'd just wounded.

"You'd better go now, Micah. You obviously have more important things to do."

She reached for the door and slowly closed it between them.

CHAPTER 17

☾

On a sigh, Jenna closed her eyes, sinking into the tub of warm water and frothy suds Brock had drawn for her in their quarters.

The worst of her lightheadedness had passed, but she couldn't seem to shake the strange buzzing sensation that had taken up residence in her skull. For the past week, it had been a nearly constant companion, as if a hive of bees had gotten inside her cranium and were checking out the place.

Considering all of the other "unadvertised specials" that came with the tiny piece of alien biotechnology the Ancient had embedded inside the back of her neck, this latest development seemed like more of an annoyance than cause for alarm.

Even still, it was beginning to drive her a little batty.

Brock's strong palm lighted gently against the side of her face as he took a seat on the edge of the tub while she soaked. "How's the water?"

"Perfect." She opened her eyes and found him gazing down at her in concern.

"Do you want me to take the buzzing away?"

She shook her head. "It's nothing. I'm okay, I promise."

Her big, tough mate who was so skilled at combat and lethal force was also gifted with the ability to soothe human pain with his touch.

Although she was evolving into something very different from basic Homo sapiens since the attack she'd suffered a couple of decades ago, at her core she was still human. And no less head-over-heels in love with the handsome Breed male currently stroking his thumb over her cheek.

Brock's dark brown eyes held her with so much tender affection it made her heart skip a beat. She turned her face into his caress and pressed a kiss to the center of his palm.

"Why don't you join me in here?"

His gaze flared with amber sparks. "You know I'll never turn down an invitation to get naked with you. But first you need to close those pretty peepers and relax for a little while. You've been putting in a lot of hours in the archive room. Maybe it's catching up with you."

She gave him a reassuring smile. "That's probably it."

He reached around her to pick up a fluffy terrycloth towel, folding it into a pillow for her. He placed it behind her head, then leaned down and kissed her. "I'll come back and check on you in fifteen minutes. I'm right outside if you need anything."

She nodded, practically purring as he traced the pattern of an alien dermaglyph that swirled and looped around her breast.

Settling back against the large soaking tub, she watched him get up and leave, his long-legged stride carrying him back into the spacious living area of their private residential quarters.

Brock was right, she probably was spending too much time working on her journals and diagrams lately. It was hard to explain to him or anyone else the obsessive kind of determination she had to record everything she saw in her visions. It was as much an outlet for her to try to make sense of the memories she saw through the Ancient's eyes, as it was a compulsion to give the Order and their future generations an understanding of who their otherworlder fathers had been—even if those truths weren't always easy for them to hear.

Life . . . or death?

The words came to her like a ghost from the past, the voice deep and airless. Inhuman.

She hadn't heard that airless growl in years, yet it was one she would never forget. It filtered into her head now as if the creature from her nightmarish ordeal in Alaska were standing right next to her now. She knew that was impossible. The Ancient was dead. His words were only an echo across time, like the memories he'd left planted inside her.

Life . . . or death? How it shall end depends on you.

She hadn't understood what he was asking of her in those terrifying moments before he removed the alien bit of biotechnology from his arm, then held it out to her with an impossible choice.

Life or death? You must decide right now.

Jenna closed her eyes and slid down into the soapy water, submerging her head in the hopes it might douse the Ancient's voice and ease the odd sensation still droning in her skull. She popped back up a moment later, sluicing the suds off her face.

She'd left a washcloth on the edge of the tub somewhere. Eyes shut, she reached out blindly with her hand to search for it.

Instead, she felt the sudsy water and tub disappear and her fingers closed around the cold grip of a four-foot blade she now carried at her side.

No, not her fingers.

Not her blade.

She opened her eyes and found herself alone in the dark, moving through the middle of a dense boreal forest. Frost-coated leaves crunched underfoot, the ground hard with the coming of winter. A frigid wind blew through the branches of tall pines and spruces, making her breath steam as it rolled through her parted lips.

Not her lips. His.

The Ancient who had altered her life completely all those years ago.

Like a video reel of his memories playing in her senses, she got a front row seat to random snippets of his life and the things he did while he lived, from the mundane to the sadistic and everything in between.

This was a new one.

He trudged through the tight clusters of trees, heading somewhere with purpose. Overhead, a thin crescent moon hung in the cold, cloudless night sky as the sound of his brisk footsteps stirred small animals to bolt from their shelters and scatter into the underbrush.

He moved deeper into the forest, his gaze trained on a peculiar formation of dark boulders several hundred yards ahead in the darkness. As he neared it, his pace slowed to a stop. Blade in hand, he pivoted to scan his surroundings, his preternatural gaze piercing the taiga, searching for signs of trouble or evidence that he was being followed.

Nothing but silence answered.

Not the halfling sons they had sired, only to have the bastards scorn them as monsters and begin to turn on them as enemies.

There was nothing around him but endless dark, and the bracing wind.

Sheathing his blade, he swung back around to approach a large formation of giant rocks that jutted out from the uneven ground. One of the boulders, the bulkiest of the group, stood taller than even his seven-foot height. It was that one he went to, pausing in front of it. He pressed his large, glyph-covered hand against the stone. A vibration hummed beneath his palm and fingers, and Jenna realized it was taking a reading of his DNA.

With only the subtlest shift in the air, the entire rock formation vanished. In its place was an enormous craft that was nothing of this Earth. One end of the huge ship had suffered severe damage. Irreparable, by the look of it.

The Ancient pressed his palm to another panel on the exterior of the craft and waited for the lock to release. A large hatch lifted. He ducked beneath it to step inside.

The interior was sleek and bare and cool, with corridors going in several directions. He followed one that led deeper into the ship. He paid no attention to the banks of lifeless controls and nonfunctioning monitors.

There was no need, after all. The vehicle that had carried him and seven other scouting conquerors from the dark planet they called home would never make another journey again. Those who had survived the crash that dropped them on this primitive rock centuries earlier were marooned here forever now.

Forced to skulk in the shadows like vermin while the sun baked the planet a full half of every day.

They should have been kings here, as they were back home.

Instead they were hostages of the light.

He moved farther inside, heading for the section of the craft where a collection of eight long containers were situated. Several of the pods were empty, their clear lids left open. The two others held the bodies of the crew mates they had lost to the killing sun's rays shortly after their arrival.

Long accustomed to their presence, he hardly glanced in their direction. Instead, he moved to the ship's command center, where he tapped a darkened dashboard panel. It was here that the heart of the craft continued to beat. The technology powering this last surviving system was robust enough to outlast all life on Earth, but the primitive life forms existing here could not be allowed to have it.

Neither could the race of otherworlders who had also claimed a corner of this planet as their own. Atlanteans, they called themselves. Light-worshipping immortals whom he and his comrades intended to hunt into extinction.

They had already made significant strides in that direction.

His people would not rest until they had finished them all, including their queen.

And if it seemed he and his comrades might fail in that mission, they had agreed on a final solution.

He tapped a panel on the wide dashboard and a familiar diagram illuminated below the glass. His fingers moved over the schematic in a specific pattern, leaving a trail of light where his touch had been. It was a code he was entering, some kind of sequence.

A detonation sequence.

After he was finished, he glanced at his forearm. Beneath his glyph-covered skin, a rice-sized object lit up with a pulsing, bright glow that echoed the one still beating like a living heart on the dashboard.

The Ancient's interest moved on to something else now. The press of his palm unlocked a small compartment of the console beside him. It opened for him, exposing a container the size of a child's lunchbox.

Its sturdy, silver metal sides gleamed, and he handled it as if it were made of fragile glass.

He lifted the lid, his low chuckle the only sound in the silence of the ruined ship.

Inside the box rested a pair of egg-shaped crystals infused with unearthly, mercurial light.

Enough energy to destroy Atlantis. Enough to wipe out all existence on Earth.

Life . . . or death?

How it shall end depends on you.

Shock jolted through Jenna. The vision dissolved as she sat up and let out a scream.

"Jenna. I'm here." Brock was at her side as soon as her eyes flipped open. "What just happened?"

"The Ancient."

She pushed herself out of the water, practically falling out of the tub before he caught her and held her upright.

"The two Atlantean crystals the Ancients took from Atlantis," she gasped. "I saw them, Brock. I know where they are."

CHAPTER 18

She had never been a bigger fool.

The worst of it was, she had no one to blame but herself for the hurt she was feeling.

After all, she had been the one who sought out Micah last night, not the other way around. She had gone into the weapons room to find him with clear eyes and the full understanding of what might happen if she pushed a dangerous male like him.

She had presented herself—and her heart—on a silver platter. She shouldn't be surprised that he would take both and never look back.

Mine.

That's what he'd growled against her lips as she had surrendered herself to him so completely. She thought he'd meant it. She had stupidly, blindly, believed that he was feeling something more for her than just the physical need they had both been unable to deny.

After the passion they'd shared last night, the way they fit so perfectly, the way Micah looked at her with such intense possessiveness and desire, she felt as though she belonged to him and only him. She'd nearly convinced herself that in spite of the terrible way they'd met in the Dreamscape, destiny actually had played a hand in bringing them together.

She didn't realize the claim he'd been staking came with an expiration date.

Humiliation still burned in the pit of her stomach long after he'd left to meet with Lucan. Phaedra stowed her unpacked travel bag inside the walk-in closet of her guest room, trying to put the whole confrontation out of her mind.

The look of shock on Micah's face when she'd informed him she would be staying in D.C. for an undetermined time replayed mercilessly in her head. He had been more than surprised or disappointed. He'd stared at her as if the floor had just opened up beneath him. As if he couldn't have gotten any worse news than the fact that she was not going to be boarding a flight for Rome at any moment.

If nothing else, it was better that she understood how he truly felt, even at the cost of her pride. She'd lived far too long and endured more than enough loss than to waste another moment feeling like a fool for allowing herself to get swept away on thoughts of fate and destiny.

Maybe Micah had it right after all.

Maybe their shared dream of the white doe in the Deadlands was just that. Nothing but a dream.

Maybe soul bonds and fated mates really were just a lot of Atlantean love-and-light bullshit.

She scoffed under her breath, reaching for her phone to call Sia. She needed to feel grounded in something real again, and a chat with her friend was a good place to start.

Before her fingers had closed around the device, a knock sounded on the other side of her closed door, followed by Zael's voice.

"Phaedra, are you in there?"

She set down the phone and went to let him in. "Is anything wrong?"

"It's Jenna. She had a vision a few minutes ago." The former Atlantean royal guard was never one to rattle, but there was no mistaking the gravity in his voice. "Jenna saw the two missing crystals—the ones that were used to destroy Atlantis. She knows where they are."

Phaedra couldn't hide her shock. "You mean she saw them in the Ancient's memories?"

Zael gave a grim nod. "There's more, Phaedra. She's in the war room downstairs. Lucan has called everyone in the command center to come and hear what she has to say."

She nodded, hurrying after Zael. They were the last to arrive in the war room. Gideon and Savannah were gathered around the large conference table with Gabrielle and Brynne, Tegan and Elise, as well as Sterling Chase and his daywalker mate, Tavia. Micah, Darion, and Jax were on the other side of the table beside Nathan and Jordana. Micah glanced Phaedra's way as she entered with Zael and they took their places near everyone else. As for the rest of the room, all eyes were trained on Jenna, who stood beside Brock at the end opposite of Lucan.

"Go ahead," the Order's leader said, giving Jenna a grim nod. "Tell them what you just told me."

Phaedra listened in astonishment as Jenna went on to describe what she'd witnessed through her strange connection to the Ancient who had left his indelible mark upon her before his death.

No one said a word as she relayed detail upon detail of the Ancient's trek through a dense boreal forest where the alien wreckage had lain undisturbed for millennia, cloaked on the ground where it had crashed.

She told them about the advanced circuitry and systems the Ancient had tried unsuccessfully to repair, about the life pods and the pair of bodies stowed in the rear of the ship.

And then she told them about the two Atlantean crystals the Ancient had stored there too. How he had programmed a detonation trigger into the ship, then synced the protocol with the biotechnology chip he'd carried in his forearm.

The same chip that now resided in Jenna.

"Life or death," she murmured. "He made me choose one or the other that night in my cabin. He wasn't just talking about my life, though. With the crystals on board that ship, then should it blow, he was talking about eradicating every living thing on this planet. That trigger was set to detonate if and when his life ended. Now, I'm the one carrying that burden."

"Holy hell." Lucan's deep voice was airless, his face stark with obvious dread.

It was a feeling clearly shared by everyone in the room, Phaedra included. No one said anything for a long moment, the entire gathering gone silent under the weight of what Jenna had just revealed.

Brock gathered her against him, his arm around her shoulders as tender as his gaze. "I'm never going to let anything happen to you, Jenna. I made you that promise a long time ago, before we understood anything about that damn chip and what it might do to you."

"Yes, you did," she whispered, leaning into his embrace. "I've never been this scared of what he did to me, though. The changes in my body, the awful visions . . . I can handle all of that. Making me live with this is the cruelest part of his assault on me."

Brock kissed the top of her head. "We're in this together, baby. If you're scared, you just keep holding on to me. I'll always keep you safe."

"It's been more than two decades since the last Ancient died," Gabrielle interjected quietly from her place next to Lucan.

"Yes, it's been twenty years since he died," Savannah said. "But he was held captive in Dragos's lab for about twice that long, and before then Dragos had kept him in another kind of prison for centuries."

Elise nodded. "Which means Jenna's vision must have taken place during the time before. All the way back to the Middle Ages."

Tegan bit off a low curse. "So, that fucking ship's just been sitting out there abandoned and forgotten in the Deadlands somewhere all this time."

"That would be the best scenario," Lucan replied.

Gideon exchanged a grim look with him. "Considering the way our luck's running lately, I don't think we can count on best scenarios."

Nathan's cool gaze flicked to the Order's leader. "There's no such thing as luck, only opportunities to be won or lost."

"Well, this is one we can't afford to lose," Sterling Chase said, abruptly standing up and starting to pace. "We need to know where that ship is before anyone else gets to it."

"Damn right we do," Micah agreed. "Since I'm the only one of us who's been in that godforsaken stretch of scorched taiga, I should be the one to go."

Phaedra didn't want to acknowledge the way her heart lurched to hear him volunteer to return to the area that nearly killed him once already. She had to remind herself that he wasn't hers to worry over. Besides, she didn't think she'd be able to stop him from taking on such a dangerous mission even if she tried.

That didn't mean her heart had to agree.

"There is another thing to consider," Zael said soberly. "We may not be the only ones searching the Deadlands in pursuit of the crystals."

Sterling Chase glanced his way. "You think Opus might have intel on the crystals?"

"That's one possibility," Zael hedged.

"But you're talking about a greater threat than that." Darion's deep voice drew everyone's attention. "You're talking about Selene."

Zael nodded. "How long ago was it that the swath of Siberian land was rendered uninhabitable?"

"Ten years," Lucan replied. "There was some kind of disaster in the region—nuclear or chemical, it was never fully determined. Whatever happened, it scorched hundreds of thousands of acres into a toxic wasteland. To this day, no one has taken blame for the event."

"You think it was Selene?" Tegan asked Zael.

He gave a mild shrug. "If she suspected the crystals might be hidden in the area, what better way to dissuade anyone else from getting curious than to cast the entire region into forbidding Deadlands?"

Jax arched a brow. "If she made the Deadlands a decade ago, can we be sure she hasn't already retrieved the crystals from the ship?"

"She hasn't," Phaedra said. "The crystals are still out there. Nothing else could have created the blast of light that hit Micah and his team."

"You're certain of that?" Lucan asked.

She nodded, feeling Micah's eyes trained on her from across the room. "There is no doubt in my mind. I would never mistake their power for anything else."

"That's not all," Jenna added. "The ship is protected, not only by the cloaking field that masks it to the outside world, but by a lock that can only be opened with a DNA key. I saw the Ancient press his hand to a digital panel as he arrived at the ship. It read his DNA before the portal unlocked for him."

Gideon leaned forward as she talked, a smile edging his mouth. "So, you're saying even if Selene knew where the ship might be, she wouldn't be able to get inside?"

"That's right."

"Then, unfortunately, neither will we," Tavia interjected from the other side of the table. "Of all of us in this room, Brynne and I are the closest genetic link to the Ancient's DNA. Not even you Gen Ones are purer than us," she said, glancing at Lucan, Tegan, and Nathan.

Jenna nodded at Tavia. "You're right. There's no Breed male or female here, be it daywalker, Gen One, or otherwise, who would be able to unlock the Ancients' ship. The fact that Micah and his team triggered some kind of defensive reaction from the crystals when they got too close makes me certain they've been integrated with the ship's perimeter security. Our best—possibly only—way to get inside is by faking out the system. There's only one of us here who can do that."

Brock let out a low growl. "Jenna. I know what you're going to say, and it's out of the question."

She glanced at him. "I'm the only one who might be able to do this."

"And if you can't?" Scowling, he ran his hand over his head. "Come on, baby. There has to be another way. You know what's at stake now if you're wrong. You saw it for yourself—that thing is rigged to self-destruct if anything happens to you. If the crystals really are inside, then any detonation is going take the whole fucking planet along with it."

"That's exactly why I have to try. I'm our best shot at getting inside that ship."

Low conversation rumbled among everyone gathered. Even Phaedra had her doubts that Jenna should risk any amount of harm. Still, her courage was remarkable.

Lucan stared at Jenna. "You sure you want to do this?"

"I have to do it." Her hazel eyes were determined. "If we're going to send anyone into the Deadlands to look for the crystals, you're going to need me to come along."

"Then I'm going to be there too," Brock said, his voice flinty with resolve. "You go, I go."

She reached up, cupping his jaw in her hand. "Lucky you, right? This is what you get for falling in love with a cyborg freak of nature."

"You know I've been all in from day one," he said, smiling. "No regrets, sweetheart. Not for a second."

"I'm in too," Micah said, the finality of his statement leaving no room for argument. Not from his parents or Lucan.

Most certainly not from Phaedra.

"Send me along with them," she said, turning her attention toward Lucan. "If the crystals are still inside the ship, I may be the only one who can extract them without being harmed. I can also provide protection for the team, as I did last night."

"And alert Selene and every other Atlantean to our location while you're at it?" It wasn't Lucan who objected, but Micah. She didn't have to look at him to feel his disapproval practically burning her from the other side of the table. "We can't risk tipping our hand, no matter the cost."

"We can bring in some daywalkers," Jax suggested. "Aric and his new team in Boston are only a few hours away."

"Atlantean light isn't the same as ultraviolet," Zael pointed out. "Daywalkers will be just as vulnerable as anyone else, Breed or human."

"Or any other Atlantean," Phaedra added, feeling the need to caution him as well.

He nodded. "Phaedra's right. Any team going near those crystals is going to need the kind of cover only she can provide. Without her, this mission is over before it begins."

Lucan listened in pensive silence, then he exhaled a low sigh. "As if we don't have enough shit to deal with already. We still need to respond to Opus for that fucked up UV ambush last night. Gideon, how are we doing on that lead you're working on?"

"The software worm is ready to roll. All I need is a backdoor into one of Opus's encrypted networks and it's showtime. Once we infiltrate their digital link, there'll be nowhere left for them to hide."

"We need to make it happen," Lucan said. "Jenna's just given us a new Priority One but I don't want us taking the heat off Opus for one bloody minute. Every one of those bastards is going down, and I mean hard."

"For Eli," Jax said, giving a solemn nod.

Every voice in the room echoed the vow. "For Eli."

Lucan dropped his hand on the table like a gavel. "All right. I'll make my decision on the Deadlands team and we can start putting that plan into motion."

With nods and murmured agreements, everyone got up and started filing out of the war room. Phaedra waited until the rest of the group had exited before she stepped out to the corridor.

Micah was waiting for her after everyone else had gone, a look of barely couched fury in his eyes. "What the fuck do you think you're doing?"

She hiked up her chin. "I don't know what you mean."

"Like hell you don't." Sparks flared in his lavender irises. "You're not going on this mission."

"I believe that'll be up to Lucan, not you."

She started to walk away from him, but Micah caught her by the wrist. The tips of his fangs glinted with his sharp, indrawn breath. "Goddamn it, Phaedra. I can't have you out there with us."

"Why, because you still think I'm hiding an allegiance to Selene? I suppose you still hold me responsible for what happened to your team in the Deadlands too?"

It hurt more than she expected to think he might believe she was his enemy. Didn't he know she would never do anything that would put his life—or anyone else's—in peril?

"Let me go, Micah." When he didn't relax his grasp, she pulled her arm free and started walking away.

"Phaedra." A curse exploded out of him. Next thing she knew, he was standing right in front of her. "You say you can't be harmed by the crystals, but what if you're wrong?"

"I'm not wrong."

"But what if you are? Have you ever tested your theory? The Ancients decimated the Atlantean population using those two crystals. Not even you could have held back the tsunami that took Atlantis down." He stared at her, his gaze intense and unwavering. "Now, according to Jenna, those same crystals are somewhere on board a ship that's rigged to blow to kingdom come. If we get this wrong and that fucking ship explodes, the crystals won't protect you." His deep voice lowered to a choked snarl. "I won't be able to protect you, either."

She swallowed, unwilling to imagine the potential annihilation, the total loss of life. The destruction of the entire planet itself. None of that changed the fact that she had to be part of the mission to retrieve the crystals. If anything, what he said only made her role that much more crucial.

"I don't need anyone's protection. And you have nothing to say about what I do or what I choose to risk."

"I think I've got more to say about it than anyone else."

"Why? Because you fucked me?"

His head reared back, eyes blazing. "That's one reason, yes."

"What other reason could you possibly have? Don't tell me it's because we met in the Dreamscape. I'm well aware of what you think about that. In fact, I'm starting to agree with you, Micah. It is bullshit. And I'm not your problem."

He let out a harsh, humorless laugh. "You've been my problem from the instant I saw you, Phaedra. Meeting you in the Dreamscape had nothing to do with that."

She steeled herself to the look of resignation in his smoldering eyes. She had already let herself believe she meant something to him. She wasn't going to play the fool for him again.

"I will be going back to the Deadlands to help locate the crystals," she stated evenly. "And then I'll be going back to Rome, whether the Order agrees or not."

CHAPTER 19

Phaedra must have packed and repacked her meager belongings half a dozen times in the several hours that had passed since her heated exchange with Micah.

She wouldn't be able to avoid him forever. Tomorrow, she would be departing with him and the rest of Lucan's hand-selected team for the expedition to the Deadlands. She had been informed they would be flying in the Order's private jet to an airport in Kazakhstan where a smaller, specialized aircraft would then transfer them to the Siberian interior under the cover of night.

Phaedra glanced at the outfit of black fatigues and combat boots Brynne had brought by for her a short while ago. The warrior's garb was a far cry from Phaedra's supply of simple dresses, jeans, and light tunics originally intended for her short holiday at the colony.

There was a part of her that couldn't wait to try it on.

But there was another part of her that didn't want to rush the dangerous mission into the Deadlands. Not only because of what they might encounter in their search for the pair of missing crystals, but also because when they returned—successful or not—she would be leaving the Order behind and resuming the life that waited for her in Rome.

When she'd called Tamisia to explain this further delay in her return, she was surprised to hear her friend's enthusiasm for working at the shelter. Not that it should have surprised her. During the many weeks Sia had assisted at the shelter after her fall from grace with the colony, Phaedra had witnessed her kind heart and tireless work ethic firsthand.

The shelter's residents couldn't be in better hands while she was away . . . or, should the Deadlands mission go horribly wrong and she was unable to return at all.

Phaedra didn't want to consider all the ways they might fail, yet it didn't keep the troubling thoughts at bay. Her soul was heavy with dread, not only for the task that lie ahead, but also the inescapable truth that no matter what fate might have intended for Micah and her, reality was pulling them apart.

After pacing restlessly in the confines of her room, she decided what she really needed was some air. She needed a few minutes to cleanse her spirit and her mind, and there was always one sure way for an Atlantean to do that. With the sun already on its descent toward nightfall, she had only a few spare minutes to soak up what she could.

Phaedra left her room and walked to the cozy courtyard garden she'd found that morning.

It was empty now, and she stepped outside to the inviting patch of solitude.

Golden afternoon sunlight bathed the stone patio and the colorful flower beds beyond. She walked out to the middle of it and tipped her head back, her arms spread wide beneath the warming rays. The light fed her cells as much as it nourished her soul. She drank up all she could, breathing slowly, letting the sun's gifts wash over her.

She didn't know how long she stood there. It wasn't until she heard the soft crunch of gravel under a delicate foot that she opened her eyes and looked around her.

"Oh, I'm sorry, Phaedra." Micah's beautiful mother halted on one of the meandering garden paths. "I was just taking a little walk. I didn't realize anyone was out here. Please, continue. I don't want to disturb you."

"It's okay." Phaedra shook her head. "You're not disturbing me at all."

"Isn't it lovely out here?" Elise gestured to the inviting grounds that surrounded them. "I often steal a few minutes to myself to visit the gardens whenever Tegan and I come here. Being around so much glorious nature helps me think." A small smile curved her lips. "It also helps me stop thinking, when I'm worrying over things I can't control."

Phaedra exhaled a shallow sigh. "I understand."

"I'm sure you do." Elise approached her, nodding toward a small bench situated near a tall, fragrant rosebush. "It's too nice to go inside so soon. Would you like to join me for little while?"

"I'd love to."

They sat together in comfortable silence for a moment, both content to simply admire the golden light as the sun began to sink below the tops of the trees. It wouldn't be long before it was dark and the warriors inside the command center began suiting up to start their patrols.

"It's not easy loving a member of the Order," Elise remarked, her gaze still fixed on the setting sun. "Knowing they're always surrounded by violence and death, realizing there is the very real possibility of losing them every time they go out on a new mission. It never gets any easier."

"No," Phaedra said. "I can't imagine it does."

"But loving someone is always a risk. It's the most important one we can ever take." Elise turned her head, her expression soft. "Don't you agree?"

"I suppose it is, yes."

Elise stared at her for a long moment, then slowly nodded her head. "I understand you'll be leaving tomorrow with the team heading back to the Deadlands."

"We leave in the morning."

"Look after him for me."

Phaedra held the entreating lavender gaze that was so similar to Micah's. "Of course, I will. I'll do whatever I can to shield everyone on the team."

"Micah would hate that I'm afraid for him. I know I shouldn't be. He's every bit as skilled and fearless as his father. He always has been so much like Tegan." Elise's smile faltered a little. "I suppose that's exactly why I worry."

There was something reassuring and grounding about the idea that a six-and-a-half-foot-tall, intimidating wall of muscle, might, and lethal power still had a mother who fretted over him.

Phaedra worried too.

She worried that Micah was so intent on pushing people away, one day he was going to wake up and realize he had no one left around him. Or worse, his refusal to let anyone in might send him down a dark path from which he might never find his way back.

Phaedra feared for him for many reasons, but right now, it was her heart she needed to protect.

"I don't plan to return with the Order after we complete our search for the crystals, Elise. My place is in Rome, not here. I'm not afraid of what Selene might try to do to me, and I will never allow myself to be used to harm the Order or any of its members."

Elise nodded, studying her in pensive silence. "You care deeply for my son, don't you?"

Phaedra glanced down at her hands. "Our lives are too different."

"Because you're Atlantean and he's Breed?"

"No. Because I don't think I have the courage to let myself fall in love with him."

"Oh, I see." Elise's placid tone indicated she understood far more about that than she was letting on. Phaedra looked up and saw a quiet sympathy in the other woman's eyes. "I was adopted as a child by a well-respected, affluent Breed family in Boston. I had everything I could possibly want or need. Eventually, I fell in love. I became the Breedmate of a good man, and we had a son together, Camden. I thought my life was perfect. It was perfect . . . and then it all fell apart. Quentin was killed in the line of duty. Several years later, our teenage son fell victim to a destructive narcotic that turned him into a blood addict. Before I knew it, Camden was dead too."

"I'm so sorry," Phaedra said, reaching out to squeeze Elise's hand.

She had the sense there was a lot more to both the story and the pain Elise was sharing. The fact that she felt comfortable sharing what she had made Phaedra feel an instant friendship with her, a kinship that touched her deeply. It was a feeling Phaedra regretted because she knew this, too, would be lost to her when she returned to Rome.

Elise placed her other hand over Phaedra's. "When I met Tegan, I couldn't have been in a worse place emotionally. Our lives couldn't have been more different. Was I terrified to let myself fall in love with him? You have no idea. But I would've been even more afraid to live my life without having taken that chance."

Phaedra nodded. "It's been a long time since I've risked opening my heart to love. I was married many years ago, Elise. He was human. He was a gentle man. A safe man."

"There's no shame in wanting those things in a mate."

"I know. But I didn't really find my purpose until he was gone. A violent man killed Niccolo when he got between the man and the woman he was beating. After that, I opened my house to women and children in need of protection. I've been doing it ever since."

Elise smiled. "You're a bit of a warrior yourself, Phaedra. And I think your heart has more courage than you know. I can see why fate would want to put you and Micah together."

Phaedra shook her head. "I'd always believed in destiny because my parents had that rare bond. But if it was fate that made Micah and I meet in the Dreamscape, shouldn't it be easier for us to be together?"

"That's not something I can tell you," Elise said, her voice gentle. "The only place you'll find that answer is in your own heart. You and Micah both."

She rose from the little bench, glancing over her shoulder as the last of the warming rays dipped below the tree line. "The sun will be gone soon. Are you coming inside?"

"In a few minutes," Phaedra said.

"All right." Elise folded her arms against the rising chill and quietly returned to the mansion.

Phaedra sat there, watching night begin to fall, and wondering if maybe she was the one who was going to wake up one day and realize she had pushed everyone out of her life.

CHAPTER 20

☪

"Need any help with that?"

Micah briefly looked up at the sound of his father's voice. "Nah, I'm good."

He had spent the past couple of hours in the weapons room selecting the equipment he planned to take with him tomorrow when he and the rest of the Deadlands team would be leaving.

Mostly, he'd been doing his damnedest to avoid running into Phaedra after their clash outside the war room.

If he didn't steer clear, he was only going to make her despise him even more than she did already. Or, worse than that, he might do something stupid like get naked with her again or tell her he didn't want her returning to Rome. Not because the Order had deemed it best strategically that she stay under their watch, but because he wasn't ready to let her go.

Neither option was any good for her.

And he couldn't allow himself to get any deeper when it came to his feelings for her, either.

He had set his course a long time ago. He couldn't step off it now, when the Order was taking hits from all sides and his duty as a warrior had never been more vital.

Opening a cabinet that held an array of blades, he chose a pair of curved daggers and tested the feel of them in his hand. He put one of them back, and the other went into a sheath on his weapons belt.

"Your mother is worried about you heading back to the Deadlands," Tegan said as he stepped farther into the room. "She won't say it to you, but I think you should know."

Micah grunted. "It's only an expedition. Locate the ship, search for the crystals, and, hopefully, bring them back with us."

"Sounds easy enough," Tegan said, but the skepticism in his voice wasn't missed on his son.

"If we run into problems with Selene or anyone else, I'll be ready for them."

"You're still itching for that fight, aren't you?"

It wasn't really a question. His father knew him too well to wonder if Micah still burned with the need to avenge his fallen team. Hell, they were more alike than either one of them probably cared to admit.

"The five lives ashed in those woods demand justice. I'm not going to stop craving that payback if I have to spend the rest of my days looking for it."

"You sure you're not looking to punish yourself?" Tegan stared at him. "You didn't kill your men, Micah."

He scoffed. "Didn't I? We went into the Deadlands on my command. I'm just as responsible as anyone else."

"If you hadn't gone in, we'd have no idea the crystals might be in the Deadlands somewhere. Jenna's vision of the ship in a forest could have placed them anywhere. It was you and Phaedra who provided the connection we'd be missing otherwise."

Micah frowned. "We can't be certain the crystals are there."

"Phaedra doesn't seem to have any doubt." His father's unblinking gaze was inscrutable. "She's a remarkable woman. It's too bad she's got a civilian life waiting for her return. We could use someone with her incredible power, not to mention her courage."

Christ, Micah couldn't argue that. Phaedra would be—and was, in fact—an invaluable ally to the Order. But courageous and powerfully gifted or not, seeing her on the front lines of their battles was the very last place he wanted her to be.

"She's going back to Rome after we finish in the Deadlands," he stated as tonelessly as he might give a count of the rounds on his weapons belt.

"I thought Lucan decided she should stay under our protection."

"He did. Phaedra doesn't care what the Order thinks is best. She's leaving."

"I see," Tegan said.

Micah scowled. "I'm going to ask Lucan to talk with Lazaro Archer, see if he can put one of his men on her security, even if they've got to do it covertly."

Tegan grunted. "I thought you might be the one to volunteer for that duty."

"No." The denial tasted sharp on his tongue. "I've already got a job to do. I intend to return to black ops as soon as possible, if Commander Reichen will have me. Not as captain of another unit, but on my own."

Tegan stared at him. "That would be a mistake, Micah. You're a good leader. Better at it than I was or ever could be."

The praise was unexpected, but it was the reflection in his father's eyes that took him aback even more. There was pride there. Even admiration.

It took him a moment to find his voice. "I made a promise to myself that I wouldn't let my team's deaths be in vain. What other reason is there for the fact that I survived and they didn't?"

"Maybe the reason is upstairs preparing to walk out of your life. If you let her, that is."

Micah shook his head, surprised to hear that advice coming from the formidable Gen One warrior whose long shadow Micah had walked in from the time he took his first steps.

"My life is this." He motioned to the arsenal of weaponry surrounding him. "This is what I've trained to be. It's what I know, what I'm best at. My commitment to the Order has been my destiny from the day I was born."

"Yes, you are good at what you do," Tegan said. "I've seen a lot of warriors come through the ranks over a lot of years, and you rose above them all. But that doesn't mean you have to sacrifice everything else. It doesn't mean you can't be destined for other things too. Better things, like Phaedra."

Micah let go of a low curse and ran his hand over his tense jaw. "You really think fate has something to do with the two of us?"

"I don't know. Stranger things have happened." Tegan chuckled, but there was a solemnity in his eyes. "I can't tell you anything about fate. I only know what I see in you when you're looking at her. Trust me when I tell you, son, life is for the living. I suggest you get on with it . . . before you let her walk away."

Shit. The last thing he'd been expecting was a father-and-son bonding session after a week filled with deaths and disasters. Micah didn't know what to say. Not about his unsolicited advice, or about the laser-sharp way he'd seemed to drill right into the heart of what Micah feared even more than failing at his promise to his team.

He feared the possibility that he might be falling in love with Phaedra.

Fuck, it was more than a possibility.

The hollow ache in his chest when he saw the hurt in her eyes today—hurt he had caused—had not dissipated in the hours since. It had only carved in deeper when he thought about her returning to the life she'd left behind in Rome.

She wasn't even gone yet and he missed her already.

Tegan cleared his throat. "I'll let you get back to your work. Lucan wants everyone in the war room in twenty minutes to review patrol missions for tonight's sweep of the city."

Micah nodded. "I'll be there."

Tegan dipped his chin in response, then pivoted to leave.

"Hey... Dad?" He paused as Micah called after him, swiveling his head to look over his shoulder. Micah swallowed, then gave his father a smile. "Thanks."

Some of the stone that seemed to enclose Tegan cracked with the fond look he held on his only son. "Whatever you decide to do, I'll support you. And I'll be proud of you. I always have been."

Their gazes locked and held for a long moment, then his father resumed his walk toward the corridor. Before he reached the threshold, the comm units both he and Micah wore on their patrol fatigues began to buzz with an incoming notification.

"That's Lucan," Tegan said, frowning as he glanced down to read the display. "Holy shit. Everyone's needed in the war room on the double."

Micah fell in beside him, their boots chewing up the distance to the war room where the rest of the Order's on-site members were arriving at an urgent clip too.

There was no need to ask why they had been summoned.

Two large monitors on the wall were filled with the same breaking news report from a swank society gala taking place downtown. A stricken-looking anchorman stared into the camera from his studio as he described the situation inside.

"Again, this just in, we're getting reports that a private function being held at the city's historic opera house has been overtaken by a group of heavily armed individuals. Our sources inside the building tell us the men are holding close to fifty hostages, among them visiting diplomats, business leaders, and government officials."

Lucan shot a look at Gideon. "We got any intel on this gathering?"

"I'm checking now." Data filled another monitor in the room, halting on a page that displayed a roster of Who's Who in D.C. society. "Ah, fuck me. You're not gonna like it. The guest list for this gala? It's almost entirely Breed."

"Jesus Christ," someone hissed.

The news anchor kept talking, resting his finger against the receiver in his ear. "What's that? All right, we're getting new information. Apparently, the armed men inside have a message they want to deliver. Is someone getting me that video link?" The anchor paused for a moment, then nodded at the camera. "Okay, stand by and we're going to have that feed in just a moment—"

The broadcast abruptly cut away from the studio. Filling the screen now was a live video feed of a twitchy looking man with a pock-marked face and a leering grin. He stood in a small office somewhere inside the theater, holding an assault rifle in his hands. He wasn't alone. Half a dozen more gunmen stood there too, clustered in a circle around the perimeter of the room.

Kneeling in front of them in a bespoke suit festooned with a colorful sash and a lapel full of medals was a Breed male with his hands raised in surrender.

"Son of a bitch." Gideon raked his hand over his disheveled hair. "That's the ambassador from the Breed nation in Ireland."

"Yes," Lucan growled.

"What the fuck?" Darion paced closer to the twin TV screens. "Those assholes holding him are human."

Micah realized it at the same time a cold knot of dread settled in the pit of his stomach. "And those guns are the same kind that opened fire on us outside Slake last night."

"UV," Jax confirmed grimly.

Scarface grinned into the camera someone was holding in front of him. "Opus Nostrum has a message they want to deliver personally to the Order, specifically to Lucan Thorne."

Silence fell over the war room at the thug's mention of the terror group. The Order's wounds from the ambush suffered last night were still fresh. Now this.

"Opus demands Lucan Thorne's immediate surrender. If he does not comply, we have instructions to start executing hostages. He has ten minutes to get here. After that, every five minutes we have to wait to take the Order's leader into custody, we're gonna ash another one of these fanged bastards."

Micah glanced at Lucan, who stared at the monitors with a look of cold menace in his eyes.

"You can't do it, Lucan." Tegan's voice broke the awful quiet in the war room.

"He's right," Chase agreed. "There's no negotiating with Opus."

Brock nodded. "Especially not when they're armed to the teeth with goddamn UV rounds."

On screen, the gunman's ugly face broke into a manic grin. "One dead bloodsucker every five minutes. And just so you know we're serious, here's a little teaser."

The handheld camera swung away from Scarface and toward the pleading ambassador. Then gunfire cracked from all of the Opus foot soldiers, bullets ripping into their target. The liquid UV went to work instantly. Mercilessly. The Breed victim's screams of agony filled the war room, before falling into a hideous silence as his body was consumed.

Then the screens went black.

CHAPTER 21

☾

Phaedra hardly recognized the woman staring back at her in the full-length mirror of her guest room.

On a whim, she'd given in to the urge to try on the outfit of black fatigues and combat boots, expecting to feel awkward in the warriors' attire. Instead, she felt . . . empowered. She felt a little badass.

More than a little.

She could hardly tamp down the amused smile that quirked her lips as she smoothed her hands over the form-fitting, long-sleeved black shirt. The rugged black pants Brynne had given her were a couple of inches too long, so she'd tucked them into the tops of her lug-soled black leather boots.

She laughed when she imagined what Tamisia's reaction might be to seeing her normally reserved, tea-loving friend dressed like a full-fledged member of the

Order. All that was missing was a weapons belt bristling with daggers and firearms.

An urgent knock sounded on the other side of her closed door, accompanied by Brynne's voice, brisk with alarm. "Phaedra? Are you here? I need to speak to you. It's urgent."

She hurried over and opened the door. The daywalker's gaze took her in with a swift up-and-down. If she had questions about her change of attire, it didn't appear there was time to ask them.

"Something awful's happening in the city. A gang of Opus followers have taken control of a building downtown. They've got hostages—Breed dignitaries and other civilians. They say they're willing to release them, but they want Lucan in exchange."

"Oh, no." Phaedra's heart sank.

Brynne's expression took on an even graver look. "Phaedra, there are more than a dozen of them that we know of, and they're all armed with UV rounds. Just a moment ago, they ashed one of the dignitaries on live video. They've threatened to kill one hostage every five minutes they have to wait for Lucan's surrender."

Phaedra swallowed. "What can I do to help?"

Brynne flashed a brief, but relieved, smile. "I was hoping you'd say that. Come on."

They ran through the snaking corridors toward the weapons room. Nearly all of the Order were already assembled and gearing up to roll out. Gideon announced he would be monitoring the operation from headquarters and holding the fort along with Savannah, Gabrielle, Jenna, and Elise. The hallway buzzed with hurried talk of unit strategy assignments and the jostle of weaponry as the men headed for the elevator that would take the teams down to the fleet garage.

Through the hustling crowd, Micah's gaze found Phaedra. She couldn't pretend she didn't feel the electricity of his penetrating stare, or the spiral of longing it woke inside her. Nor could she deny the jagged bolt of fear clutching her heart as he and his comrades hastened to prepare for another UV battle with an enemy force that had already slain one of their own.

Zael and Jordana, also dressed in black like everyone else, intercepted Phaedra and Brynne as they arrived at the edge of the activity. Their small group was quickly joined by Sterling Chase and his daywalker mate, Tavia.

"Phaedra's in," Brynne said. "Do we have our plan of attack?"

"Yes," Chase said, "and our odds of pulling it off just got better." Turning a rushed nod and a smile on Phaedra, he then signaled to Lucan and the others that they were ready to move out. "Let's go. We'll lay out the details on the way."

They split up into two units. Chase, Tavia, and Nathan took Phaedra, Brynne, Zael, and Jordana in one of the Order's Rovers. Micah and the rest of the warriors followed Lucan and Tegan into a huge black SUV that looked as heavy and indestructible as a tank.

With Nathan at the wheel, Chase doled out instructions for their covert support strategy their team would be providing for Lucan and the others.

Phaedra prayed the plan would work. While Lucan feigned his intent to publicly surrender in front of the building, his warriors would be taking up positions around the location at various points of entry. Meanwhile, Phaedra's team would be infiltrating the theater from the roof and service entrances with the goal of protecting the hostages and eliminating as many UV gunmen as possible until the Order could come in to safely rescue the captives.

"Everyone ready?" Chase asked after Nathan had parked the vehicle a couple of streets behind the historic building. At the round of assenting replies, he pulled his black knit cap over his light-colored hair. The tips of his fangs gleamed as he spoke. "All right, let's get this done."

They jumped out of the vehicle on silent feet and made their way through the darkness to the back of the old brick theater. Chase indicated the zigzagging fire escape where Zael and Brynne were to take Phaedra up to the roof. As they began the climb, Nathan wrapped his arm around Jordana, then leapt from the ground to a second-floor railed balcony that circled the building.

Phaedra held her breath as she watched Nathan stealthily unlock a pair of French doors then slip inside with his Atlantean mate. Chase and Tavia leapt to the balcony on the opposite side of the building and went in from their assigned position too.

Zael was the first onto the roof. Brynne hopped up from the top of the metal fire escape, then they both reached down to grab Phaedra's hands and hoist her up beside them.

A chill night wind skated across the roof tiles, carrying the sounds of the video news crews and curious spectators who had gathered in front of the building after the reports of trouble inside. People on the ground out front started to shout when they spotted Lucan approaching by himself.

"That's him!"

"Holy shit, Lucan Thorne's actually giving himself up!"

Phaedra exchanged a smile with her two partners. The Order's risky plan was moving right on schedule. Now all they had to do was execute their end.

Alongside Zael and Brynne, she stole toward the roof's access door Chase had shown them on the digital blueprint they reviewed on the way from headquarters. Brynne mentally disabled the lock and the three of them slipped inside. On silent feet, they moved onto one of the many catwalks two stories above the stage.

The performance had been halted in a hurry, as evidenced by the knocked over stage props and vacated orchestra pit with its scattered chairs in complete disarray. The sounds of panicked voices and crying drifted in from the open doors of the vestibule in the front of the theater, where the gunmen had apparently corralled their hostages.

"Let us go," one of the captive Breed males pleaded. "There's Lucan Thorne now. You have what you wanted, you bastards!"

"Not yet, we haven't," came the smug reply. "All you bloodsuckers stay put and do what you're told. We want a nice, big crowd out there before we open these doors. Anyone gets brave and we're gonna ash another of you just for the fun of watching you fry."

Brynne eyes flashed with rage at the human's threat. She looked at Zael, giving him a short nod. Then she stepped off the edge of the catwalk and dropped to a crouch on the stage as silent as a ghost. She started moving swiftly toward the doors to the vestibule.

Zael listened to the earpiece connecting him and Brynne to the rest of the Order's teams and Lucan. He nodded, then whispered to Phaedra. "Everyone's inside. I'm going down to help Brynne get the hostages back into the theater. Tavia and Jordana are closing in from their positions too. Once we have them all inside, then you can shield—"

"Hey, bitch!" A menacing shout came from the theater below. "How the fuck did you get in here?"

Zael's face blanched. "Brynne."

His palms lit up with power—at the same time the crack of a gunshot split the air.

Phaedra sucked in her breath. The UV bullet wouldn't have given Brynne anything more than a puncture wound. That is, if she hadn't been fast enough to dodge it.

And if her Atlantean warrior mate hadn't unleashed a ball of light from his palms at the same instant.

The human slammed against the wall from the impact of Zael's assault, dead even before his broken body hit the floor.

Panicked screams went up from the crowd being held in the vestibule.

The men holding them there showed the first signs of alarm as well. One of them poked his head into the theater.

"Fuck! Biggs is down," he shouted into a mouthpiece clipped to his jacket. "Repeat, Biggs is—"

He didn't get the chance to finish. Brynne let a dagger fly. The blade now buried in the gunman's chest silenced him as he crumpled to his knees, then fell in a lifeless heap.

"Hit the switch!" another of the Opus lackeys bellowed from the vestibule. "Hit the goddamn switch now and unlock the doors. We gotta get the hell outta here!"

"What's going on?" Phaedra asked.

Zael shook his head. "I don't know. I don't like it."

Smoke started to filter in through the ventilation system. It was bitter and strange, and tinted an odd, reddish color. It billowed in more rapidly now, big clouds of it beginning to fill the theater from all angles.

Zael's receiver rasped with an incoming status from the Order's teams. "We've got gunmen fleeing for the basement exits over here," Darion's deep voice reported. "We're going after them."

"Get out! Everyone, get out," Brynne shouted into her comm unit. She started coughing as the smoke fell down toward her. She vaulted back up to the catwalk, her irises lit with amber sparks. "They're pumping Red Dragon inside here."

"Damn it," Zael growled. "I need to get you out of here. Phaedra, you too. Back to the roof with us. Now."

Down below in the vestibule, the Breed civilians and diplomats started choking on the narcotic fumes. The snarls and animal sounds they made as the Red Dragon absorbed into their bloodstreams put a chill in Phaedra's marrow.

Their captors having abandoned their posts, the Breed hostages had no one to keep them inside their makeshift pen.

One big male in a tuxedo burst out of the vestibule and into the theater. He tilted his head up, spotting them on the catwalk. His lips peeled back, fangs bared in rising Bloodlust. On a roar, he sprang into the air.

Phaedra's palms went hot with her alarm. She released the bolt of light that built in her hands, knocking the snarling Breed male back to the floor.

Another one stormed inside behind him, letting out an unearthly bellow.

"Let's go!" Zael shouted, hurrying away with Brynne huddled close to him, her face buried in his chest to keep from breathing any more of the toxic air.

"What about the rest of them down there in the vestibule?"

"They're a lost cause. The Red Dragon has them now. If I don't get Brynne out of here, it'll have her too."

Phaedra started running with them, panic like cold lead in her breast. She only hoped Micah and the other warriors heeded Brynne's warning. Part of her couldn't bear to leave without knowing for certain they had fled the building.

She hesitated, needing to know he was safe. If anything happened to him—

The thought cut off abruptly as an iron grasp sank into her shoulder and yanked her back.

On a sharp cry, she wheeled around . . . and found herself staring into the savage, bloodthirsty amber eyes of the tuxedoed Breed male she should have killed with her power.

His jaw hung open, revealing razor-sharp fangs dripping with pink-tinged saliva. "Where do you think you're going, pretty?"

~ ~ ~

Micah's vision burned raging amber when he saw the newly turned Rogue in the fancy tux catapult himself up to make a grab for Phaedra.

The Breed male may have been a gentleman when he arrived at the theater event, but the clouds of Red Dragon pouring in through the ventilation system had made him a slavering animal. Putting him down would be a mercy at any time now that he was Rogue, but the male had made the mistake of threatening Phaedra and for that, his death was guaranteed.

Micah leapt up behind him with not even a second to spare and drove one of his long titanium daggers into the back of the Rogue's neck. The metal was toxic to a Breed vampire caught in the throes of Bloodlust.

The body dropped off the catwalk, plummeting to the stage below.

"Micah." Phaedra stepped forward on a small cry. "I didn't want to leave without knowing you were okay."

"I'm good now," he said, relief at finding her unharmed pouring through him. He kept his words to a minimum, trying not to breathe any more of the poisonous dust. Grabbing her around the waist, he used every measure of Breed velocity at his command to flash to the roof's open exit and bring Phaedra outside to the fresh night air.

Zael and Brynne were there too. The Atlantean had his hand resting on his mate's back as she doubled over and tried to expel the Red Dragon fumes from her lungs.

"Is she all right?" Micah asked.

Zael gave him a grim nod. "She will be once I get her out of here. Where are the rest of the teams?"

"Clearing out of the building as fast as they can." Micah was still holding on to Phaedra, his arms unwilling to release her. "Are you okay?"

She nodded. "You saved my life."

He cocked a crooked grin. "I still owe you one. Don't make me have to pay it back."

She smiled, reaching up to caress his face. Christ, it felt good to be holding her, to be looking into her eyes, even under shitty circumstances like these.

Tegan's voice sounded in Micah's ear. "You safe?"

"Yeah. I'm on the roof with Phaedra, Zael, and Brynne." Micah cursed under his breath. "Things are fucked up ten ways to Sunday inside. That Red Dragon they pumped into the vents has turned all the hostages into Rogues."

As if to underscore the grim situation, a loud crash sounded from the front of the theater building, followed by a burst of terrorized screams and general hysteria.

"Ah, fuck," Tegan hissed. "Those sons of bitches let them loose. We've got Rogues pouring out of the building down here."

"I'm on my way." He glanced at Phaedra, reluctantly letting her go. "Stay here with Zael. I will come back for you."

He took off before she could argue with him, which he was certain she was about to do.

Peering down from the rooftop at the front of the theater, he watched in horror as a mob of close to fifty Breed vampires rushed at the news crews and spectators.

Left with no alternative, Lucan, along with Tegan, Brock, Darion, and Jax had formed a line and were taking out the charging Rogues as they poured out and ran blindly to attack human prey.

A hail of 9mm gunshots rang out. Titanium blades flashed, spilling the blood of the Breed civilians who, only minutes ago, had been among the Breed nation's most prominent citizens and dignitaries.

All of it captured on live video being broadcast around the city, if not the whole world.

Another goddamn setup.

Another direct strike on the Order from Opus Nostrum. One that had now painted not only the warriors, but the Breed as a whole, as savage monsters who could only be controlled by death.

Micah cursed as he watched the carnage worsen. Then he drew the hand-tooled titanium blade his father had given him when he first joined the Order, and he stepped off the edge of the roof into the fray.

CHAPTER 22

By the time it was all over, the stone steps outside the old theater looked like a battlefield.

Blood stained the ground and pavement. The bodies of dozens of dead Breed civilians lay where they had fallen in their elegant evening attire. Some of the Bloodlust-crazed victims had been taken down by Order gunfire, others felled by daggers like the one Micah still held in his hand as the warriors regrouped in the aftermath of the slaughter. The titanium bullets and blades were already devouring the flesh and bones of the dead. It would only be minutes before the corpses would be gone completely.

Lucan's eyes blazed as he pivoted to the news crews, their spotlights still shining over the carnage, cameras still broadcasting the grisly scene all around the world.

"Haven't you got enough fucking pictures? Get out of here."

The snarled command sent the reporters and video crews scrambling to collect their equipment and race to their vehicles.

Micah glanced across the way where Darion and Jax were holding one of the Opus gunmen. The group of humans had scattered like rats after they sent the Red Dragon into the theater, but they hadn't gotten far. Micah's comrades had killed all but one. Scarface didn't look so smug now that he was caught between two Breed warriors and left to answer to the Order all by his lonesome.

As for Micah and the rest of his team, it was only by some miracle that none of the warriors had inhaled enough of the heinous narcotic to turn them Rogue. If not for Brynne's early warning, this bad night could have ended up even worse.

And then there was Phaedra.

Micah could hardly contain the urge to run to her. She stood beside Zael, Brynne, Nathan, and Jordana as he and the rest of the Order rounded the building to meet them at the vehicles. Her private smile as she watched him approach cracked something open inside him. He had been telling himself he could hold her at arm's length, but all of that fell away now.

She took a halting step toward him, then paused, uncertain. He had no such reservations. Closing the distance in a few swift strides, he pulled her into his arms and held her tight.

He felt the eyes of his comrades on him, but he didn't give a damn. Let them stare.

He released her only so he could tip her chin up and press his lips to hers for an all-too-brief kiss. There would be time for more of that later. He intended to make certain of that.

"Let's roll out," Lucan said. "Micah, you ride with Zael. We've got to make room for this piece of shit who's going to tell us everything he knows about Opus."

Scarface struggled against the restraints locked around his skinny wrists. "I don't know anything," he whined. "I wouldn't tell you even if I did."

"We'll see about that," Darion said, flashing his fangs in the human's face. "Come on, asshole."

He yanked Scarface toward the rear of the Order's SUV and shoved him inside. They all climbed into their respective vehicles and headed back to the command center.

Phaedra stuck close to Micah for the duration of the drive. He'd never known a braver woman, but he could feel the depth of her shock in the small tremors vibrating through her. What happened tonight was enough to rattle even the most seasoned warrior. He hated like hell that she'd been there to witness any of it.

Everyone began to disperse once they arrived at headquarters. There would be reports to provide to the JUSTIS about what occurred, not to mention all of the countless public relations and political fires that would have to be put out now that video of the incident was circulating to all corners of the globe.

On top of that, the Order now had an Opus asset they needed to take apart for intel.

Micah would have loved a front row seat for Scarface's interrogation, but he had something more important to tend to.

He dropped a kiss to the top of Phaedra's head where it rested against his shoulder. "I'll walk you to your room."

His arm sheltering her, they made the trek in silence. Once inside, Micah closed the door and followed Phaedra to where she paused near the bed.

She stared at him, her pretty golden gaze troubled. "The Order's enemies are never going to let up, are they?"

He shook his head. "Not until we stop them. And we will."

"How?"

"We'll keep fighting. That's what we've done from the very beginning."

"How do you do it, Micah?" Her eyes were soft on him, as tender as a caress. But there was pain in them too. Pain for him. "The violence that never ends. The ugliness you have to face every time you put on your patrol gear and go out there. All the hideous things you have to bear because of your gift. How do you keep it from consuming you?"

"I deal with it," he said. It was an automatic response he was so used to giving, it slipped right past his lips now, too.

But she deserved more than that.

Reaching down for her hand, he traced his finger over the silken skin of her palm. He could feel her power thrumming there, the warmth of the light she carried within her, not only as an Atlantean, but as a unique, singularly extraordinary woman.

"What I've done, Phaedra, is built a wall. Stone by stone, one layer on top of another. Nothing could get past it. Nothing ever did. No has one ever gotten inside. Then I met you."

She stared up at him, inhaling a shallow breath. "I thought you only had room for the Order, for your duty to their cause."

He nodded. "If you had asked me that several days ago, I would've agreed. I would've told you that's the only way it could be."

"I'm asking you now, though, Micah."

He brought his other hand up and stroked her cheek. A storm of emotions swamped him when he thought about Phaedra and what she meant to him. All the words he wanted to say jammed in his throat, inadequate and clumsy.

It would take him a lifetime to express what she had come to mean to him in only a handful of days.

He scowled, frustrated at his lack of eloquence. "I don't want you to go back to Rome."

"That's where my life is," she said softly. "That's where my work is."

He felt his brow furrow deeper. "It's not safe for you there. Not without someone to protect you." She started to draw back and he knew he was fucking things up. "I know you're strong, Phaedra. I know you're smart and resourceful. You're the most courageous and powerfully gifted woman I've ever met. Yes, you're immortal, but that doesn't mean you can't be hurt . . . or that you can't be killed." The very notion gripped his heart in a vise. He blew out a curse as he caressed her beautiful face. "I thought about that tonight, when I saw that Rogue going after you. If anything had happened to you—if you had gone into that theater tonight and not come out . . ."

She turned her cheek toward his palm. "I felt the same way about you, Micah. I don't know what I'd do if that Red Dragon had poisoned you like it did those other people. Or if it had been you the other night along with Eli when—"

He gave a harsh shake of his head. "I'm here."

Lifting her chin on the edge of his hand, he lowered his head and kissed her. Need erupted inside him, but he kept his mouth gentle on hers, unwilling to mistreat her the way he had the last time he'd gotten close enough to kiss her.

She moaned as he moved his hands to her delicate shoulders.

No, it wasn't a moan. Not one of pleasure, that is.

Hearing her sharp little intake of breath, he realized she was in pain.

He pulled back at once, releasing her. "You're injured."

"No. It's nothing."

"Let me see."

Taking the hem of her black shirt in his hands, he carefully lifted it over her head. His gaze lit on the purple bruise in the shape of four large fingers and he ground out a low curse, recalling how the Rogue at the theater had grabbed Phaedra as she was trying to get away.

The edges of his vision burned amber with rage.

"It's okay," she assured him. "Micah, I'm okay."

He couldn't take his eyes off the dark outline of the Rogue's fingers. It was impossible for him to ignore how her blood was gathered there, just beneath the creamy velvet of her skin. Being Breed, his hearing was acute enough to detect the flutter of her pulse, which sped to an even stronger tempo under his hungered stare.

He hadn't fed in days. Too long, especially considering he was little more than a week out from serious injuries of his own.

But what he felt as he watched Phaedra's heartbeat throb in the graceful curve of her neck and shoulder, he wasn't thinking about satisfying his need for nourishment or healing.

His thirst was something more than that.

The thirst to claim her.

To make her his alone, for as long as he lived.

Reining in all of the needs he felt when he looked at her, he lowered his head and lightly kissed the unmarked skin around her bruise. She would heal soon enough, and while he knew his beautiful Phaedra could withstand far greater pain than what the Rogue's punishing grasp had inflicted, Micah wanted to take away every hurt she suffered. Now and in the future.

Forever, if he had his way.

He lifted his face to hers, blown away by the affection shining in her eyes.

And the desire.

Holy hell, her desire sparked a fire in his blood now. It ignited all of the need he'd been fighting since he brought her into the room.

Cupping the back of her head, he pulled her toward him and brushed his lips over hers. Her soft gasp against his mouth was raw with invitation. Drawing her closer, he slid his tongue inside her heated kiss, then gently nipped his way along her jaw line. She said his name on a broken whisper. He answered with a deep growl that unfurled from somewhere deep within him.

"Christ, I've needed to kiss you again," he murmured, his breath harsh and heavy. "I've needed to touch you again."

Her shuddering little moan spurred his desire. He reached between them to caress her breasts, his fingers searching out the front closure of her bra and snapping it open. He groaned against her mouth as he stroked and kneaded the soft, buoyant swells and the pearled peaks of her nipples.

Breaking their kiss, he bent so he could bring one of the cherry-red buds up to his mouth. Her head fell back as he suckled her, taking care not to abrade her tender skin with the sharp points of his fangs. The temptation to bite down and pierce the soft flesh—to claim her by blood—was nearly overwhelming.

On a snarl, he pulled back. "You look so fucking hot dressed in combat gear. I've been hard all night just from seeing you like this. Now, all I want to do is strip you out of it."

She gave him a saucy smile, her lovely face flushed with arousal. "I want you naked too."

They moved with urgent, determined fingers, unfastening buttons and buckles and laces, tugging at fabric and zippers. When the last of their clothing and boots lay on the floor, their hands found each other.

Questing fingers on bare skin.

Soft curves pressed against hard planes.

Hot, mingling breaths and a wild, escalating desire that had both of them shaking with the depth of their mutual need.

Micah brought her over to the large bed and followed her down onto the mattress. He stroked her gorgeous face, then let his fingers trail along her shoulder and onto the beautiful terrain of her body.

Her touch moved all over him too. He shuddered at the feather-light feel of her fingertips as she traced his *dermaglyphs*, anticipation wringing him as tight as a coil as her exploration continued downward, where the thick jut of his erection rose between them.

Her grasp wrapped around his shaft and he bit off a guttural curse at the arrow of pleasure that shot through him. Then she began to stroke him, her fingers moving from root to tip, making his blood surge in his veins.

He took her mouth in a hungry kiss, bucking his hips in time with the tormenting tempo of her caress. He slid his hand down her silky curves and over the pliant angles of her body, memorizing every velvet inch of her on his way to the juncture of her thighs.

She sucked in a sharp breath as he slid his touch over the delicate patch of dark curls between her thighs. She was drenched for him already, her clit a tight knot at the top of her tender folds. He moved his thumb in teasing circles over her flesh, then slipped one finger inside her.

She moaned and arched as he penetrated her, her tender walls constricting around his finger as he teased her with what was yet to come.

"You feel so soft and wet," he uttered thickly. "Fuck, I need to taste you."

Shifting lower on the bed, he moved between her legs and spread her open for his hungry gaze. Her sex glistened, as ripe and succulent as a peach.

On a growl, he lowered his head and took her juicy sweetness into his mouth. Where his fingers had been a moment ago, now it was his tongue drinking in every tender part of her, savoring every nuance of her pleasure.

He didn't let up until she came, her throaty cry exploding out of her as she shuddered and broke against his mouth.

He could have devoured her all night, but his own needs were a demand he could no longer deny. He moved so he was kneeling between her parted thighs, her legs wrapped around him. She stared at him with pleasure-drunk eyes, her hands reaching for his stiff cock.

She stroked him with both hands, her touch as greedy and possessive as her immortal gaze.

"Please," she gasped jaggedly. "I need you to fuck me now, Micah."

He wasn't about to make her ask twice.

Shifting position, he covered her with his body and entered her slowly, pushing all the way to the hilt in one long stroke. She sucked in her breath as he filled her, then moaned in protest as he began to withdraw.

Together they watched their bodies joining, then their eyes found each other and locked as they settled into a deep, perfectly matched rhythm.

"You're mine," he growled as he rocked into her. "I've known it all along. Even fate knows you're mine, Phaedra."

"Yes," she answered, her gaze fearless and without a shred of reservation as she stared up at him. "I never knew it was possible to love someone so deeply, so quickly. But I do, Micah. I love you."

It was more than he was prepared for her to say. Everything about this woman was more than he was prepared for. She was his. God help her, but he belonged to her too.

On a low growl, he took her mouth in a rough kiss. Passion had him in flames now. He was savage with the possessive need that swamped him. He was ravenous with thirst for this woman.

His woman.

As they kissed and moved together, he could hear the strong beat of her pulse ticking at the side of her neck. The sound grew, filling his head as he pounded into the welcoming heat of her body.

Christ, the temptation of that vein was too close to his mouth, too close to his fangs, which throbbed with the demand that he make her his in the most primal, permanent way he could.

On a curse, he broke their kiss and turned his head away from her, his breath heaving.

Phaedra's hands lit tenderly on both sides of his face.

Slowly, she brought his blazing amber gaze back to her. Understanding simmered in her shining golden eyes. "I want it too, Micah."

His reply was wordless, just a rough snarl of warning. She shook her head, her stare locked on him.

"I want this. I want you to do it." She tilted her head, giving him full access to the delicate column of her neck. "Drink from me."

Ah, fuck. Her plea burned away what little control he had where she was concerned.

She clung to him as he drove deeper, unable to hold back on the desire he had for her . . . or the thirst.

"I don't ever want to let you go," he confessed thickly, then lowered his head and sank his fangs into her yielding flesh.

She cried out, flinching in his arms. For one awful instant, panic gripped him. It was too late for doubts now; there was no turning back what he'd just done.

But she didn't have any doubts. He could already taste that truth as the first hot rush of her Atlantean blood surged into his mouth. He had only ever drank from humans, so the electric taste of her came as a shock.

Holy hell, it was more than a shock. It was a revelation.

There were no words powerful enough to describe the flood of heat and energy and light that poured into him from her vein. She lit him up from within, her blood as sweet as nectar and as pure and bright as heaven and the stars combined.

He drank more of her, unable to get enough.

He would never be able to get enough of Phaedra. He'd known that even before his bite had now cleaved her to him in an unbreakable bond for as long as either of them lived.

And through that bond, he could feel the overwhelming wave of her oncoming release.

Her pleasure intensified his own, until he could no longer hold out against the force of it.

With a hasty swipe of his tongue over the punctures he'd made, he sealed her wound and began thrusting into her in a blind, desperate rhythm. She raked her fingernails over his shoulders as the first crash of her climax slammed into her.

He was right behind her, his release exploding inside her. Holding her in his arms as they both gave themselves over to the power of their connection, he felt invincible.

He felt complete in a way he never imagined he could.

And he couldn't stop moving inside Phaedra. Whether he was still hard or hard again, he didn't know. He only knew he needed to feel her around him, for the rest of his days and nights if fate would allow it.

Eventually, he would have to let her sleep. The morning was going to arrive too soon, bringing with it the mission to the Deadlands.

But for now, there was only room for pleasure.

Kissing Phaedra again, he pressed her beneath him for more of what they'd just shared.

CHAPTER 23

☾

Phaedra woke at the edge of night and daybreak.
It was her favorite hour, when the moon and stars still shone in a sky that hung suspended between fading indigo and the lavender shades of dawn.

Wrapping a thin shawl over the ankle-length nightgown she'd slipped into before leaving her guest room with Micah yet asleep in her bed, she padded barefoot through the mansion to the courtyard garden she loved.

A layer of fog swirled in the crisp morning air. Like puffs of feathers, the mist danced over the stone tiles of the patio as she stepped outside. The gardens beckoned, their beds of red roses, pink dahlias, and gold chrysanthemums glowing like jewels against the dew-covered greenery.

She walked along the stone path, smiling to herself as she thought about the hours she'd spent with Micah. She never dreamed she'd find this kind of happiness, this kind of fullness.

Absently, she brought her hand up to the side of her neck where he'd drunk from her. To think she had long considered the Breed to be a dangerous race, one she should fear as the offspring of the marauders who had decimated her people. She hadn't held the Order much higher.

Now, she had given her heart to one of them. She had given Micah more than that. Her blood. Her bond. Her soul.

She felt giddy in love, and as she strolled deeper into the fragrant gardens, she could hardly curb the joy that blossomed inside her. A small giggle escaped her lips as she tilted her head up to watch the stars twinkle defiantly in their last hour before morning would come and chase them away.

She was so engrossed in her own contentment she didn't realize she wasn't alone in the garden.

Feeling a soft stir in the air, she broke out of her reverie and looked to the path ahead of her.

A handful of yards away, the white doe stood in the swirling fog.

Phaedra drew in her breath. "Are you real?"

The ethereal animal pivoted away and trotted deeper into the milky mist. She followed, hurrying to catch up as the fog thickened and the tall hedges turned one way, then another.

Breathless, Phaedra rounded a corner—and there she was.

No longer the white doe, but a woman illuminated in a soft glow.

She was tall and graceful, with luminous, gentle golden eyes ringed in thick lashes and a face so beautiful it almost hurt to look at her. The long dark hair Phaedra remembered was now snowy white shot with silver.

"Mother?"

She smiled. "Oh, Phaedra."

A choked cry caught in Phaedra's throat. "It really is you?"

When she took a step forward, her mother took a step back, giving a sorrowful shake of her head. The thin outline of light that surrounded her trembled with her movements. "You cannot touch me, dear heart. I can only maintain this form from a distance, and only for a little while."

Phaedra swallowed past the knot of emotion in her throat. So many emotions. Shock, amazement. Regret that she couldn't walk up to her mother and embrace her, if only for a moment.

"It was you. The white doe in my dreams all those nights—in Micah's dreams too, leading both of us into those barren woods." Phaedra stared at her, feeling a niggling confusion begin to seep into her heart. "It was you in the Dreamscape?"

Sindarah nodded soberly. "It was the only way. I had to reach you somehow. I had to take the chance."

"What do you mean? Take what chance?"

It took her mother a moment to say the words. "Interfering with destiny."

Now it was Phaedra who drew back. Her voice came out hoarse, hesitant. "What are you saying? What did you do?"

Yet even as she asked the questions, a cold understanding settled over her.

"Phaedra," her mother said, her careful tone only making the dread worse. "The two crystals used to destroy our realm must be found . . . before their power can be unleashed again. Nothing is more important than that, do you understand?"

She shook her head. "What does that have to do with me?"

"Your father and I know where the crystals are located, but we cannot retrieve them. They've been kept somewhere no one from our realm can go. Only the Order can do that. Only their human who is no longer human."

"You mean Jenna. Only she can access the Ancients' ship because of her changed DNA."

"Yes." Sindarah tilted her head, remorse in her tender gaze. "What Jenna would not know is the location of the ship, nor had we any way to make it known to her. So, we had to wait. We had to hope that one day, the tide would turn and we could nudge fate in our direction."

"What does that mean? Nudged fate, how?"

"The warrior, Micah. When I felt his presence near the barren forest several weeks ago, I knew he was the one who could help. I could feel his honor, his courage. I couldn't reach out to him or guide him while he was awake . . . so I led him into the Dreamscape instead."

Phaedra closed her eyes as the realization sank in. "And then you led me there, too. Why?"

"Because only you would feel the crystals' nearness. You were the bridge to connect their location with the key required to retrieve them."

"You used me," Phaedra whispered. "You used both of us."

Her mother made a broken sound. "Would that there had been another way, we would have chosen it. But all our hopes rested in you, my dearest heart."

"So, the Dreamscape . . . it wasn't real at all?"

Sindarah's silence was answer enough.

Phaedra lowered her head into her hands and blew out a heartsick sigh. "We believed it. We believed all of it was true. The Dreamscape. The soul bond. Our connection to each other. None of it was real at all?"

Her mother's expression moved from confused to contrite. "I never intended to deceive you. Please, believe that. I never imagined you would think it was possible for an Atlantean and one of the Breed to share a soul bond."

"I didn't at first," Phaedra admitted. "We both were so sure it had to be a mistake . . . and now it is."

A mistake discovered too late, after she allowed Micah to drink from her only hours ago.

He would despise her for this. How could she imagine he wouldn't?

She despised herself for not realizing the chances of them sharing a bond forged by destiny was as impossible as she'd first thought it to be. It was a ruse. A lie.

Faith, she had cost him so much.

She studied her mother, thinking she should feel some amount of rage for the woman who had manipulated fate itself to bring Micah and her together for her own reasons. But she couldn't despise her mother for that. Not for anything.

And especially not when the love she had for Micah felt nothing close to untrue, despite the reason they had found each other.

That didn't mean his feelings wouldn't change once he learned the reason for their meeting.

"Micah's team was killed that night in the Deadlands, Mother. He was seriously wounded, too. Please, tell me you didn't know you were bringing them into harm's way."

"No, love. I did not realize there would be danger . . . or death. I do know the warrior is alive because you were there with him."

"But not his friends. I couldn't save them all." Phaedra thought about the road still ahead of her, the mission back to the Deadlands where the crystals—and the Ancients' dangerous ship awaited. "Why not leave the crystals where they are? Why not let the Deadlands keep them along with whatever is left of the ones who wanted to destroy us? Mother, what if we fail?"

Sindarah smiled sadly. "You are more powerful than you know, my daughter. You always were. Your gift will guide you. It will protect you. But nothing will save you or this world if the crystals' power is unleashed to destroy it."

Dread carved a chasm in Phaedra's breast. "Is that what's going to happen?"

"I do not have that answer. If I could predict the future, your father and I would still be with you."

Phaedra nodded, emotion choking her voice. "I miss you both so much."

"We will never stop loving you, my darling. You have always been our greatest pride. And I'm sorry for everything I've done." The glow outlining her form began to tremble. "I cannot stay much longer. My energy won't hold. I just wanted to see you one more time. I wanted you to know the truth."

"I'm not going to see you ever again, am I?"

Sindarah slowly shook her head, her silver-and-white hair floating around her shoulders like the fog that was now beginning to envelop her. "This is the last time I'll look upon you, but my love for you will endure forever."

Phaedra stepped forward. "Mother, wait—"

Sindarah's slender hand rose, her lips forming the word "Goodbye."

Then she was gone.

Phaedra opened her eyes and found herself naked in her bed, looking up at Micah's handsome face above her. Concern lined his mouth and put a crease in his brow.

He touched her cheek with infinite gentleness.

"Were you having a bad dream?"

She couldn't find the words to explain. She wanted to dismiss the encounter with her mother as merely a dream, but she knew it was real.

Micah smoothed her hair away from her face and shifted beside her, gathering her close to the warmth of his strong body. With his arms wrapped around her, he pressed a tender kiss to her bare shoulder.

"Everything's okay," he murmured. "I've got you now, and I won't let go."

CHAPTER 24

☾

The Deadlands expedition team departed the D.C. headquarters in the morning.

Micah still didn't like the idea that Phaedra was coming along, but he knew there was no persuading her away from it. In fact, she'd seemed more closed-off than ever in the hours before they boarded the Order's private jet with Jenna, Brock, Zael, and Brynne for the thirteen-hour flight to their first stop in Kazakhstan.

She had all but avoided him on the trip as well, except to discuss mission details with the group or pore over the sketches Jenna had made based on the Ancient's vision of the ship's interior and maps of where Jenna envisioned the vessel to be hiding.

Phaedra's distance was driving him crazy, especially after the amazing night they'd shared. Her blood still thrummed inside him, warm and electric. Through his bond to her, he knew something was bothering her.

Worse than that. What he felt from her was overwhelming regret.

Because of him?

Fuck, he hoped not.

He had left important things unsaid between them last night, chief among them the fact that he was in love with her. She had to know that even without him saying the words, but she'd deserved to hear them and not be left to wonder what she meant to him.

If she was having second thoughts about letting him drink from her, he wasn't sure he could blame her. Despite the fact that she had granted him the honor, it had been a selfish thing to do. Just as it had been selfish to presume she would abandon her life in Rome to be with him.

Now, there would be no breaking his psychic bond to her no matter where she chose to live. For the rest of his life, he would feel her strongest emotions. He would know her heart like it was his own. As for his future, she would be the only woman for him as long as either of them drew breath.

Then again, he didn't need a blood bond to guarantee that. He was hers, and always would be.

That was pretty much what he'd told his father and Lucan Thorne this morning, when he'd put in his request for a new assignment with the Order.

His gaze clung to Phaedra as she stepped away from the worktable littered with papers, maps, and schematics. With the rest of the team taking a break from their strategy talks, Micah stood up and followed her into the private lounge area of the jet's main cabin.

With little time left before they would have to prepare to touch down at the Kazakhstan airport, he couldn't take the chasm of silence that seemed to be opening between Phaedra and him. There would be no time to talk once they transferred to the military helicopter chartered to drop the team in the Siberian taiga for the long trek into the Deadlands.

Hell, he was already half out of his mind just from not being able to touch her or kiss her all these many hours of the flight.

He strode up behind her as she was gathering her long brown hair into a thick braid for the mission. The bared curve of her neck and shoulder was too great a temptation for him to resist. When he stroked his fingers along her tender skin, she ducked out of his touch and whirled around to face him.

He frowned. "I didn't mean to startle you."

"You didn't." She swallowed, glancing away from him and letting her unfinished braid swing against her back. "I'm sorry I'm so jumpy."

"Are you nervous about the mission?"

She shook her head, her brow pinched. And damn it, she still wouldn't lift her eyes to his. He caught her chin on his fingertips and guided her gaze to him.

"You haven't wanted to look at me or talk to me since we got out of your bed this morning, Phaedra. Tell me what I've done wrong."

The strangled noise she made in the back of her throat put his heart in a vise. She took a few steps away, as if she couldn't stand to be near him. "It's nothing you've done, Micah, believe me."

Ah, Christ. He really had fucked things up, then. Her face said it all. She stared at him in uncomfortable silence, her expression anguished and filled with remorse.

He lowered his voice and moved closer. "If I pushed you too far last night . . . if I asked things of you that you weren't prepared to give me—"

"That's not it. You didn't do anything I didn't want."

But he was still losing her. He could feel it through his blood bond to her. "Was it something I said, then? I shouldn't have told you I didn't want you going back to Rome. I want you to live wherever you're happiest. That's why I've put in a request to be assigned to Lazaro Archer's command center."

"Micah, you shouldn't—"

"I'm in love with you, Phaedra." He blurted the words because he needed her to hear them, before she tried any harder to push him away. "I never believed in fate or destiny, but I do now. We belong together. I feel it in my soul and I think you do too . . ."

He had more to say—a lifetime of promises he wanted to make to her—but his words evaporated in his throat when he heard her quiet sob. When she swiped at the trail of wetness that rolled down her cheek, he couldn't find his voice at all. Her sorrow was all he could taste.

"It wasn't real, Micah."

"What are you talking about?"

"Us. The Dreamscape. It wasn't real." She collected herself, but he could feel the struggle inside her. She was heartsick. She was miserable with guilt. "This morning, I saw the white doe. I dreamt I was in the garden outside the mansion. I saw the doe and I followed her. Except it wasn't the doe. It was my mother."

"Your mother?" Confusion rolled over him, even as the depth of Phaedra's regret sank cold claws into his heart. "I thought Sindarah was dead."

"She is. For all that it matters, she is. But she and my father somehow exist in the crystals too. Micah, they want the two missing crystals to be recovered. That's why we met in the Dreamscape. They needed us to help make that happen."

"What are you saying? They used us?"

She nodded, looking even more tormented. "There is no soul bond between us. It wasn't destiny at all. We were never meant to be together."

He scowled. "I don't believe that."

"It's the truth," she said softly. "We both sensed it had to be a mistake in the beginning. It turns out it was."

It felt like a hundred years ago, not a handful of days, when he'd thought of Phaedra with mistrust and suspicion. Yes, he had dismissed the idea of a soul bond with her as some kind of cosmic joke. But now?

Now, she was everything to him.

Now, his life didn't make any damn sense without her.

Phaedra stared at him for a long moment, her sorrow carving deeper—not only into her, but him as well.

"I'm sorry," she murmured. "I'm so, so sorry, Micah."

She brushed past him and stepped into the jet's small lavatory and locking the door.

He stood there for a moment, unsure if he had more fury for her parents, the crystals, or the fact that both had not only thrust Phaedra and him together but were now tearing them apart.

He didn't have long to contemplate it.

The pilot came over the speakers to announce they were on their descent into Kazakhstan. Their ride into the Deadlands—and whatever future awaited Phaedra and him on the other side—was now only minutes away.

CHAPTER 25

☾

It took more than a couple of hours before their feet touched ground in the Siberian interior. The private helicopter transport that dropped them in the taiga under the deep cloak of night had been instructed to wait for their return, no matter how long that might take.

Phaedra knew they had limited time to trek into the Deadlands and get out. If they didn't run into complications or missteps, the threat of daybreak would eventually force them back to the shelter of the helicopter to attempt their search another time.

She did not want to fail.

Even though her heart yearned for Micah, she was duty-bound as an Atlantean—as her parents' daughter—to find the crystals and ensure they could never be used against her people or anyone else on this fragile planet they all shared. Her parents had sacrificed everything to create the crystals; now, it was her turn.

She was determined, but a part of her knew only the hurt and shame she felt over Micah having been unwittingly dragged into her parents' scheme as well.

His bewildered face haunted her, as she trudged through the scorched forest with him and the rest of their team. He'd been as stunned as she was to learn they had been manipulated. As she'd feared, he was angry too.

She had waited for him to tell her it didn't change how he felt about her, but, of course, it had to matter. If he had loved her, even a little, it was based on a lie. A trick.

Never mind her mother's noble, if desperate, motivations. She had meddled with destiny and it was Phaedra and Micah who were left paying the price.

"We're getting close to the area I'd been with my team," he said, his long-legged pace slowing to a pause ahead of Phaedra and the rest of the search party.

"You're certain?" Zael asked quietly from beside the others.

With a curt nod, Micah glanced over his shoulder, his gaze lingering on Phaedra. "I would know this godforsaken stretch of woods anywhere."

So would she. The skeletal, blackened trees, the dry forest bed crunching like brittle bones under her boots . . . the darkness all around them.

She caught herself holding her breath, waiting for the ghostly white doe to appear as it had so unfailingly in her dreams before her tragic first encounter with Micah in this same area of the Deadlands. But she knew the doe wouldn't appear this time. Not ever again.

They were on their own now.

The team continued forward, pushing farther into the scorched taiga in search of the large field of boulders Jenna had seen in her vision of the Ancient's memory.

"You guys," she whispered. "There they are."

Phaedra and the rest of the group looked to where she pointed. There, all but obscured by Deadlands trees and moonlit darkness, stood a jumbled clearing of massive rocks. On the whole unremarkable, appearing to be nothing more than a natural element of the forbidding terrain.

Jenna's eyes gleamed with excitement—and certainty. "We've found it. Better let me lead the way. If I'm right, the ship will sense my DNA and let us approach."

No one asked what might happen if she was wrong. They all knew the answer to that, and Phaedra braced herself for the worst with each step they followed behind Jenna.

They made their way over to the rocks, moving swiftly and silently. Phaedra opened her senses, waiting to feel the low-frequency buzz that would tell her they were close to the crystals. All she could feel was the heavy hammering of her heart, and the slick rush of adrenaline through her veins as Jenna led the team toward the largest of the rocks.

Jenna glanced at Brock, a note of hesitation in her face now that they had arrived. "In case I don't get the chance to tell you later, you're the most amazing thing that ever happened to me."

He smiled. "Ditto, beautiful. I expect to hear it again, and often, after we all get out of this hellscape. So, open sesame whenever you're ready."

Phaedra couldn't keep her gaze from straying to Micah in those breathless few moments as Jenna stood before the boulder. If everything went sideways in the next few minutes, she would never regret giving her heart to Micah. She wanted him to know that she loved him without a shred of reservation or regret, and that she would continue loving him to her last breath, whenever that moment might come.

He stared back at her, his handsome face stern with purpose. But then, something changed in his shuttered expression. His eyes softened on her, his mouth relaxing into a bittersweet smile.

Because he knew.

Through his blood bond to her, he knew what she was feeling now without her having to say the words. He knew, and the look of yearning in his eyes told her she wasn't alone.

He loved her too.

All they needed now was the chance to start over, to make it right.

Jenna drew in a shallow breath and pressed her palm to the rock. "Oh, my God. I think it's working."

No sooner had she whispered the words, the rock she was touching vanished—along with the rest of the field of boulders.

It was just as she had described to everyone in the Order's war room. With the concealing cloak dissolved, what remained was an enormous, alien craft. One end of the huge ship was clearly disabled. The other, where the team stood, was glossy and smooth, crafted of dark metallic material that didn't appear to have any seams or doors.

But Jenna seemed to know just where to lay her hand. After a moment, a hatch that wasn't visible before silently lifted open.

No one said a word. No one so much as breathed as the cavernous interior was revealed. Dimly illuminated by small, glowing lights somewhere inside, the ship sat utterly quiet and still. True to Jenna's description, just inside the sleek main cabin of the craft, corridors branched out in different directions, all of them empty.

Micah was the first to break the awestruck silence.

"Let's get to work," he commanded quietly, taking the lead with his natural confidence and courage.

Phaedra and the rest of the group followed him inside.

"This way," Jenna said, heading for one of the bare corridors.

They followed it to another chamber of the ship, one that appeared to be the main command center. Jenna strode forward to one of the dashboards. After inspecting several of the controls, she glanced over her shoulder with a look of relief on her face.

"The detonation timer is dark. It must've lost power over time or been deactivated when the Ancient put his chip in me."

Brock blew out a breath. "Thank God."

"Do you remember where the crystals were stored?" Brynne asked her.

Jenna nodded. She indicated an area in the same chamber, while Zael walked cautiously toward the collection of cylindrical pods arranged on the far side of the large space.

"I'm going to have a look around over here."

Phaedra felt Micah's studying gaze beside her. "What's wrong?" he asked, his brows furrowed. "You're uneasy about something."

She frowned, giving him a small shake of her head. "It's just . . . the crystals. I don't feel them anywhere near here."

Micah opened his mouth to speak, but Zael's sudden curse drew everyone's attention.

He stood near the eight pods. "Jenna, how many of these were empty in your vision?"

"Six." She stopped investigating the control panels and pivoted to face him. "The others contained the bodies of two crew members who'd died of ultraviolet exposure soon after the ship crashed here."

Zael's expression was beyond grim. "Only one of these has a body in it."

"That's impossible," Jenna replied. "In the Ancient's memory, he'd been certain there were two dead comrades in those pods."

Phaedra's stomach took a sudden plunge into her boots. "That means there's one of them out there somewhere."

"Holy shit," Brynne hissed.

"We need to get out of here," Micah said. "Now."

"The crystals," Jenna said. "We have to find them."

Phaedra shook her head. "They're not here. I would feel them if they were here, and I don't."

"Neither do I," Zael said, his eyes grave. "They're gone."

Jenna raced back to the dashboard and pressed her palm against the glass. "We have to look for them, don't we? We have to try—"

Brock stilled her hand with his. "Babe, we've got to go. Now."

Micah linked his fingers through Phaedra's and in a scramble of movement, they all hurried out of the chamber with him in the lead. He skidded to a stop as soon as they cleared the end of the corridor.

"Son of a bitch."

There, on the other side of the open hatch, blocking the only exit from the craft, stood a seven-foot-tall otherworlder. Hairless, covered in dermaglyphs that ran from the top of his bald head to the full breadth and width of his bared torso, the Ancient glowered at them with blazing amber eyes. His huge fangs gleamed like daggers behind dark lips that peeled back in a sadistic smile.

Micah had a gun in his hand the instant he spotted him. He fired several shots, each one hitting its mark. Brock did the same, to no avail.

Laughing, the Ancient pressed his hand against the exterior of the craft.

"No," Jenna shouted. "Oh, no. He's going to lock us in!"

Zael and Phaedra both unleashed the power in their palms, sending twin balls of energy forward. Too late. The light hit the inside of the sealed hatch.

In less than a second, they found themselves sealed inside the ship.

Jenna flew at the door, holding her palm to the smooth metal in one spot, then another, and another. Nothing happened. The door remained closed.

Suddenly, everything got worse.

One of the dashboard panels behind them lit up. The ship started to hum to life.

"Shit," Jenna gasped. "He's reset the detonator. Oh, God, Brock. This can't be happening."

But it was.

"No," Phaedra said, steeling herself. "Micah."

She drew in a breath and suddenly he was there with her, wrapping her in his arms.

Zael and Brynne huddled into each other, too. Brock drew Jenna close, tucking her head under his chin.

The entire world seemed to fall into a hush all around them . . . right before the explosion tore through the ship in a burst of blinding, unstoppable force.

CHAPTER 26

☾

Micah opened his eyes and saw only light.

It spread out all around and above him, diamond-bright and limned with a shimmering silver glow.

The ship had vaporized.

No trace of the field of boulders that had concealed it, either.

Micah and the rest of the team now stood in a clearing, protected and unharmed by the blast that had obliterated everything in its path.

Except them.

"What the hell just happened?" Brock murmured.

"Are we dead?" Jenna asked, lifting her head off his chest to look at the dome of light covering them.

Shielding them.

They were all alive because of Phaedra.

His extraordinary, miraculous woman.

His mate, whether destiny approved or not.

"Phaedra, you did this," Brynne said, wonderment in her voice.

Zael nodded. "This is her light. She saved us."

She stood in the center of their small group, her arms raised to hold the shield of light in place, though her head was slumped toward her chest. Micah went to her, smoothing her damp hair out of her face.

"It's over, love. You did it. It's all right to let it go now."

She didn't, or couldn't, respond. Her head remained bent forward, her eyes closed against her pale cheeks. Worry settled coldly into his marrow when he realized how much the effort had cost her.

"Phaedra?" He stroked her bloodless brow. "Phaedra, can you hear me?"

Ah, Christ. She had to be okay. Reaching for her outstretched hands, he gently brought them down to her sides.

The dome shivered, then fell away like stardust. The Deadlands went dark under the thin moonlight overhead, and Phaedra slumped unconscious into his waiting arms.

"Is she okay?" Jenna asked.

"I don't know." Micah scooped her up, panic beating like a caged animal in his chest. She felt boneless . . . almost lifeless in his arms.

He threw a wild glance at the others. "I have to get her out of here."

"Go," Zael said. "We're right behind you."

Micah didn't wait. Holding her close he took off, calling upon all of his Breed genetics to speed him back to the waiting helicopter.

He hoped he wouldn't be too late.

CHAPTER 27

☾

Warm waves rolled up the sand where Phaedra walked, salty white foam sparkling on the tops of her bare feet. All around her was the scent of lemons and sunshine and sea spray.

The fragrances of home.

Not Italy. Not the mist-shrouded shores of the colony, either.

Atlantis.

The way it had been before the annihilation that swept it under the sea so many years ago.

The Atlantis she never knew, but dreamed of from the time she was a girl living in the new realm Selene had rebuilt for the survivors of the ruined paradise.

Phaedra tipped her head to the indigo-and-lavender predawn sky where the moon and stars danced in the hour between night and daybreak. Her favorite hour.

And she had seen this sky before, not long ago.

Her heart ached with yearning to be back where she belonged.

With Micah.

She didn't know how long she'd been away from him, but it felt like a lifetime. The anguish in thinking their separation might last forever was more than she could bear.

She took another step and glanced down as her toe lifted a small shell out of the wet sand. It was shimmering white and kissed with iridescent silver, tossed in the surf and weathered into the shape of a tiny heart.

The diminutive thing of beauty broke through her sorrow to bring a smile to her lips. She crouched and picked it up, folding her fingers around it as though it were a precious treasure.

When she stood up again, she realized she was no longer alone.

Micah was walking toward her from the other end of the beach.

Wearing a black T-shirt and jeans, he strode barefoot over the dusky sand, handsome and strong. The sight of him was so comforting she couldn't hold back her smile. Nor could she hold back her love.

Running to him, she threw herself into his open arms. He lifted her off the ground, and she clung to him, laughing as he held her and spun with her under the starlight.

"Is this a dream?" she asked when he set her back on her feet in the sand. "Are you real?"

He grinned. "Do I feel real?"

She ran her hands over his broad chest and muscled biceps, then she cupped his squared jaw in her palms.

"You feel real." Smiling, she rose and brushed her lips over his. "You taste real."

He stroked his fingers along the side of her face. "I've been looking for you, Phaedra. It feels like I've been searching for you all my life. Until now, I thought I'd lost you. You are my destiny. So, I came to find you and bring you home. Home to me . . . as my mate."

"But the Dreamscape—"

"I don't care if we're soul bonded or not. I don't care if fate disagrees with the fact that we're together. All I know is that I love you. I want you at my side, in my heart, in my blood. I want you, Phaedra . . . forever."

Hope burst inside her and spilled off her lips in a happy sob. "I want that, too. I love you as deeply as any soul bond could bind me to you. Deeper than that. I love you with every fiber of my being, Micah."

His lavender eyes began to glow with the light from a thousand amber sparks. "I was hoping you'd say that."

Holding her face in his hands, he lowered his head and kissed her. The feel of his mouth on hers was better than any dream. Better than any joy she'd ever known before him.

"I'm yours, Micah," she whispered against his lips.

He moaned in pure, masculine agreement. "And I'm yours."

Phaedra slowly opened her eyes. She wasn't kissing Micah anymore. The beach was gone. Above her head it was no longer the starlit, predawn sky, but a white clinical ceiling fitted with a pale fluorescent light.

She abruptly sat up—only to realize Micah was seated at her bedside, his head resting on his folded arms at the edge of the narrow mattress. He lifted his head and gave her a drowsy, sexy smile that sent spirals of heat licking through her.

Her voice came out husky and quiet. "Where am I?"

"The infirmary at the Rome command center." Although he sounded calm and in control, his words were rough with emotion. "You've been unconscious for two days. I've been waiting for you to wake up."

"The whole time?"

He slid his warm fingers along the side of her face and into her tangled hair. "Where else would I be?"

"I just had the strangest dream, Micah. I was walking along the old Atlantis shore. You were there with me."

He smiled, unsurprised. "I know. I just woke up from the same one."

He opened his other hand, and in the center of his palm was the white shell she had been holding in the dream. She stared at that tiny, iridescent heart and drew in her breath.

"Micah, I picked up that shell on the beach. I was holding it when you appeared."

He tilted his head, brows drawn together. "I picked it up from the sand. I was holding it when you appeared."

For a moment, she couldn't speak for the astonishment that poured over her. The realization of what he was saying made her heart pound against her rib cage. "The Dreamscape. We were there, just now."

His face registered surprise as well, before a look of satisfaction lit his warm gaze. "What'd I tell you? Destiny."

He set the shell down on the small table next to the bed, then moved in closer to her, bringing her into his embrace as he kissed her deeply. His love for her radiated from his touch and his lips as he moved them slowly over hers.

Phaedra could have kissed him for hours, but through her relief and elation, she recalled the terrible last moments before everything she knew turned white and silent.

She drew back from the pleasure of Micah's mouth, worry clutching at her. "Where is everyone else? Jenna and Brock, Zael and Brynne. Are they—"

"They're all fine. Everyone is safe back in D.C., thanks to you. You shielded all of us with your light." He smirked. "I'm racking up quite a debt when it comes to you saving my life."

She shook her head. "It's you who's saved mine. I don't ever want to lose you, Micah."

"Not gonna happen, beautiful. Not ever." He dropped a kiss on her chin. "Besides, it seems we've got fate on our side, after all."

"Yes, we do," she agreed, her amazement settling into an acceptance that felt so real, so right.

But there was more that weighed her heart down. She couldn't dismiss the heavy feeling of dread for what they'd discovered in the Deadlands.

"What about the crystals, Micah? What about the Ancient who's still alive?"

His face sobered. "I won't pretend the entire Order isn't concerned about that. I'm never going to lie to you. Of all the enemies we've faced over time, this new one poses a threat beyond anything we've seen before."

She swallowed and nodded, loath to imagine what an Ancient who'd intended to obliterate her and her team in the Deadlands in one fell swoop might be willing to unleash on the rest of the world. "If he's got the crystals, Micah . . . If he has any idea what can be done with them—"

"I know," he replied, without any effort to hide the grimness of his tone. "No matter what happens, we'll confront it together. You and your safety are my primary concern. That's why I'll be part of the team here in Rome effective immediately. Lazaro's already given the okay—"

"Micah, no." She shook her head. "You need to be wherever the Order needs you most. So do I. Right now, that means D.C."

"What are you saying?"

"I want to go back with you. I want to help the Order get those missing crystals. Whatever I can do to help, I'm part of this now."

He scowled as if he might refuse, but instead of arguing he moved up onto the bed with her. "You're a part of me now, too. I don't ever want to feel what I did these past two days. I need to know that you're going to be with me forever."

She caressed the hard line of his jaw, seeing the sharp points of his fangs glinting behind his lip as he spoke. "I want that too. I want all of you, Micah."

He growled, low in his throat, before he brought his wrist up to his mouth and sank those diamond-bright tips into his flesh. Then he held the twin punctures out to her.

Phaedra lowered her mouth to the wound and ran her tongue over his blood. The power in that first taste took her aback. His strength flooded her as she drank, renewing her body and washing away any doubt she'd ever had that the bond between them was anything less than soul-deep and destined.

He was the part of her she'd been missing all her life,

and as his blood roared into her senses, into her every cell and fiber and particle of her being, she knew that what they shared was eternal.

It was unbreakable.

Their bond, like their love, would outlast anything . . . even time itself.

~ * ~

Watch for King of Midnight, the final novel in the Midnight Breed series!

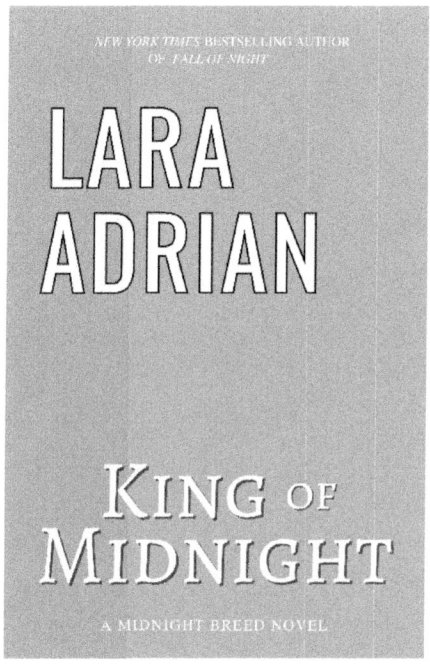

Available Fall 2021

The line between darkness and light is drawn in blood, and the stakes have never been higher.

Nothing less than the fate of the world rests in the hands of the Order, and in one Breed warrior's quest to thaw the heart of an immortal queen in the final novel of Lara Adrian's New York Times and #1 international bestselling Midnight Breed vampire romance series.

Never miss a new book from Lara Adrian!

Sign up for Lara's VIP Reader List at
www.LaraAdrian.com

Be the first to get notified of new releases,
plus be eligible for special VIPs-only exclusive content
and giveaways that you won't find
anywhere else.

Sign up today!

ABOUT THE AUTHOR

LARA ADRIAN is a *New York Times* and #1 international best-selling author, with nearly 4 million books in print and digital worldwide and translations licensed to more than 20 countries. Her books have regularly appeared in the top spots of all the major bestseller lists including the *New York Times*, USA Today, Publishers Weekly, Wall Street Journal, Amazon.com, Barnes & Noble, etc. Reviewers have called Lara's books "addictively readable" (Chicago Tribune), "strikingly original" (Booklist), "extraordinary" (Fresh Fiction), and "one of the consistently best" (Romance Novel News).

Visit the author's website at
www.LaraAdrian.com.

The Hunters are here!

Thrilling standalone vampire romances from Lara Adrian set in the Midnight Breed story universe.

AVAILABLE NOW

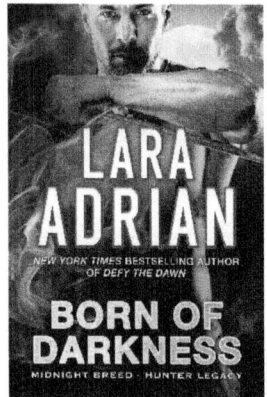

More to come!

Don't miss this sexy new contemporary romance standalone set in Lara Adrian's 100 Series!

Available Now

"Explosive chemistry, emotionally charged and utterly gut wrenching at times. I give it ten stars!!"
--*Amazon Reviewer*

"I love this book! An intense, emotional and deliciously seductive love story that captured my heart and had me absolutely captivated!"
--*Amazon Reviewer*

Thirsty for more Midnight Breed?

Read the complete series!

A Touch of Midnight (prequel novella)
Kiss of Midnight
Kiss of Crimson
Midnight Awakening
Midnight Rising
Veil of Midnight
Ashes of Midnight
Shades of Midnight
Taken by Midnight
Deeper Than Midnight
A Taste of Midnight (ebook novella)
Darker After Midnight
The Midnight Breed Series Companion
Edge of Dawn
Marked by Midnight (novella)
Crave the Night
Tempted by Midnight (novella)
Bound to Darkness
Stroke of Midnight (novella)
Defy the Dawn
Midnight Untamed (novella)
Midnight Unbound (novella)
Midnight Unleashed (novella)
Claimed in Shadows
Break the Day
Fall of Night
King of Midnight (Fall 2021)

Discover the Midnight Breed with a FREE eBook

Get the series prequel novella
A Touch of Midnight
FREE in eBook at most major retailers

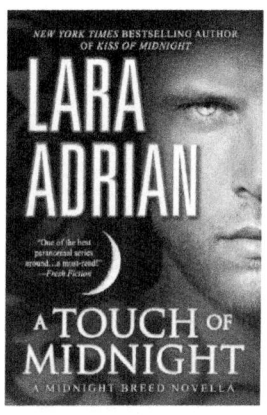

After you enjoy your free read, look for Book 1 at a special price: $2.99 USD eBook or $7.99 USD print!

Go behind the scenes of the Midnight Breed series with the ultimate insider's guide!

The Midnight Breed Series Companion

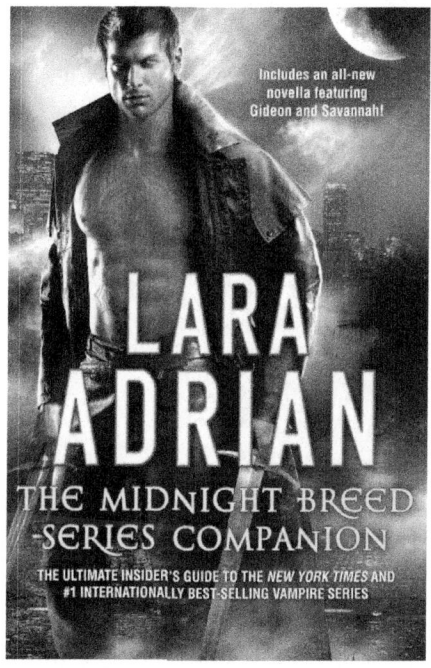

Available Now

Look for it in eBook and Paperback at major retailers.

Revisit classic moments, characters, and events in the series while exercising your memory and concentration skills with this fun new book!

Midnight Breed Series Word Search

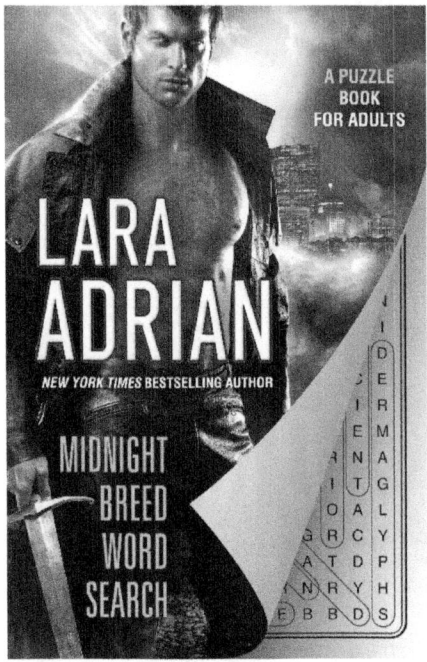

You'll find 60 puzzles, each with 24 series related words to find. Search for character names, story world lore, and other fun series trivia. Also included with each puzzle is an accompanying quote from the books, hand-selected by author Lara Adrian!

Available Now

Look for it in Paperback at major retailers.

If you enjoy sizzling contemporary romance, don't miss this hot series from Lara Adrian!

For 100 Days

The 100 Series: Book 1

"I wish I could give this more than 5 stars! Lara Adrian not only dips her toe into this genre with flare, she will take it over . . . I have found my new addiction, this series." --The Sub Club Books

All available now in ebook, trade paperback and unabridged audiobook.

Gabriel Noble barely survived the war that took his leg, but now the stoic Baine International security specialist's honor is put to the test bodyguarding beautiful Evelyn Beckham.

A 100 Series Standalone Romance

Available Now

eBook * Paperback * Audiobook

"Lara Adrian has managed once again to give us a story with heat, high emotion, and angst that touches our heart. I absolutely loved it."
—*Reading Diva*

Award-winning medieval romances from Lara Adrian!

Dragon Chalice Series
(Paranormal Medieval Romance)

"Brilliant . . . bewitching medieval paranormal series." —Booklist

Warrior Trilogy
(Medieval Romance)

 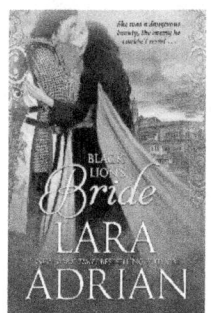 

"The romance is pure gold." —All About Romance

A dark knight abducts the daughter of his enemy as the price of her father's sins. Can the bold but innocent beauty tame the beast?

Lord of Vengeance

Available Now

eBook * Paperback * Audiobook

"A truly wonderful read."
—*All About Romance (*Grade A / Desert Isle Keeper)

Connect with Lara online at:

www.LaraAdrian.com

www.facebook.com/LaraAdrianBooks

www.instagram.com/laraadrianbooks

www.pinterest.com/LaraAdrian

www.goodreads.com/lara_adrian

Printed in Great Britain
by Amazon